INSIGNIFICANCE
HONG KONG STORIES

XU XI

許素細

Praise for *Insignificance*:

"Be prepared to see Hong Kong from the inside—its intimacies and its inhabitants' secrets are the true journey of *Insignificance*. But what made the book impossible for me to put down was the writing that bristles with intelligence and humor."

— Krys Lee, author of *How I Became a North Korean* and *Drifting House*

"An audacious, inventive and original collection: these Hong Kong stories are full of clever energy and lively strangeness."

— Gail Jones, author of *A Guide to Berlin*, *Five Bells*, and *Sorry*

"I read *Insignificance* in one gulp because it was so compelling. I loved the sophisticated wit and wry humour, the female characters who do not lend to easy stereotyping, and the sheer imaginative scope and range of the stories—from buying literal new skins, to Doghouse Rhapsodies and the ambiguous line between power and prey. Xu Xi's stories throb with fierce intelligence. They capture the history of Hong Kong and its citizens through a clear and truly original lens."

— Alice Pung, author of *Lucy and Linh*

For Louise Ho

Insignificance

By Xu Xi
Published by Signal 8 Press
An imprint of Ansh Das Media Ltd.
Copyright 2018 Xu Xi
ISBN: 978-988-77948-6-8
eISBN: 978-988-77948-3-7

Signal 8 Press
Hong Kong
www.signal8press.com

Cover image: Manuela de Gioia
Art direction: Cristian Checcanin

INSIGNIFICANCE

HONG KONG STORIES

XU XI

許素細

Signal 8 Press
Hong Kong

Other books by Xu Xi:

Chinese Walls (novel)
Daughters of Hui (short fiction)
Hong Kong Rose (novel)
The Unwalled City (novel)
History's Fiction (fiction)
Overleaf Hong Kong (short fiction & essays)
Evanescent Isles: From My City-Village (essays)
Habit of a Foreign Sky (novel)
Access (short fiction)
Interruptions (ekphrastic essays with photography by David Clarke)
That Man in Our Lives (novel)
Dear Hong Kong: An Elegy for a City (memoir)

Edited Anthologies:

City Voices: Hong Kong Writing in English (with Mike Ingham)
City Stage: Hong Kong Playwriting in English (with Mike Ingham)
Fifty-Fifty: New Hong Kong Writing
The Queen of Statue Square: New Short Fiction from Hong Kong (with Marshall Moore)

Acknowledgments:

Earlier versions of these stories have previously been published in literary journals and anthologies or otherwise made available:

"The Transubstantiation of the Ants" was commissioned for and exhibited in June 31, 1997, a visual art installation by David Clarke, Videotage, Cattle Depot Artist Village, June to July 2017; Cha: *An Asian Literary Journal* "Writing Hong Kong," Issue 38, December 2017.

"Here I Am" *The Normal School,* California State University, Fresno, California, Spring 2016.

"Mariner" *Hunger Mountain,* Vermont College of Fine Arts, Montpelier, Issue No. 20, March/April 2016.

"The 15th Annual Anniversary" *Water-Stone Review,* Hamline University, St. Paul, Minnesota, Vol. 17 October 2014.

"Kaspar's Warp" *Drunken Boat,* Issue No. 20, December 2014. ISSN#1537-2812.

"All About Skin" *The Kenyon Review KROnline,* Gambier, Ohio, Spring 2012; All About Skin: Short Fiction by Women of Color, ed. Jina Ortiz & Rochelle Spencer, Univ. of Wisconsin Press, Milwaukee, 2014.

CONTENTS

when memory shrieks

LONGEVITY'S EYEBROW

Drive all objections from your mind,
Else you relapse to human kind:
Ambition, avarice, and lust,
A factious rage, and breach of trust,
And flattery tipt with nauseous fleer,
And guilty shame, and servile fear,
Envy, and cruelty, and pride,
Will in your tainted heart preside.

Jonathan Swift: "To Stella Visiting Me in My Sickness"
(1720)

THE **last time Stella heard from Jonathan, it was six months ago in late April.** He had wanted a favor that time too, because his architect botched the renovation of his flat. *You don't hire an architect to do an interior,* she admonished, but he shrugged her off, the way he ignored all his trespasses against common sense. As usual, he overpaid. The architect was the son of someone important—the back story was unbearably convoluted—and now his space was *simply vile.* She sent him a talented designer who had just set up shop. For a reasonable fee, the young woman organized a contractor to paint over the ghastly puce, fix the expensive blinds which hung crooked and reconstruct the walk-in closet which was too large for his awkwardly small, triangular bedroom. She selected new fabrics for the living room set—pale grey—

replacing the violent chartreuse with its scarlet, oversized *fleur de lis* pattern. In return, Jonathan fucked the young woman and then "forgot" to pay his bill until Stella intervened and demanded the money. A tiresome incident, endurable only because of their longtime friendship, the way she tolerated his never-ending parade of too-young female acolytes whom he seduced and discarded with astounding vigor and regularity.

Now, listening to his preamble on the phone, she sensed the onset of another incident.

She interrupted the monologue of complaints about his department head at the university. "Jonathan, what is it you want?"

"Want? I don't want anything. This is just a how-are-you call, also to invite you over for some wine."

"Come off it. You never just call."

"Aargh, mortally wounded! What little faith you have in me, grandma."

He jabbered on. Her attention strayed to last night's un-finished sketch. She wished he would get to the point so that she could get to work.

". . . and so, if you'd find it in your heart to gift one to me, you could bring it over Friday and I'll open us this gorgeous Italian Chardonnay," he concluded.

WTF?!? shrieked across her mind, and then immediate-ly, *But why?* She said nothing. His unexpected request had stunned her into silence.

His tone slid from cajolery to sheepishness: "That'll be all right, won't it darling?"

The fire alarm in her building burst into song. "Oh no,

hear that? I must run. Call you back later," and hung up.

Of course, she did know the alarm was just a test, about which she had been forewarned.

The autumn morning was a haze of particulates. She sneezed, the romance of crisp coolness and mist a forgotten dream. A cup of hot *sau mei* in hand, she climbed the stairs to her rooftop studio. Only Jonathan would have the nerve to call so early. Up in her perch, things felt less dire.

She turned her attention back to the sketch at hand, her "Abstraction in D," the alphabet not the musical note. Although perhaps it was a note. She tried staving, but the lines daunted and evaded her vision. She tried lowercase, alternative scripts. At one point she switched on her laptop, minimized email, fooled around with typeface. She even tried a Cantonese D, code-mixed sight for sound, like 好 D meaning "better" in Cantolish. Nothing worked.

She sipped the white peony tea and set her cup down next to the inkwell. *Give up,* she told herself. There was simply no way to forget Jonathan's call.

Stella Yuen, or Gladstone-Yuen in her most cynical moments, is an artist who has achieved a global reputation for gargantuan, abstract ink drawings, although she always begins with tiny, almost miniature sketches, the details dizzying. She sketches these in her Wan Chai studio on the top floor of a six-story walk-up, above the flat that was her childhood home, the one she still inhabits, before heading to the rented loft in the Wong Chuk Hang industrial building where she stashes giant frames, easels, and ladders to complete the final art. Forget the back story implied by her name, except to know that it was her father who raised her, with modest means, in this very district on Hong Kong Island after Mother swanned her way back to England and the estate in Dover, having slummed long enough in the colonies and fucked her share of bohemian natives. Stella's father was a calligrapher till his death, one of the best. Ignore her illegitimacy. The problem at hand is Jonathan, who believes that an annoying persistence will succeed, Jonathan Bracken, who always must get whatever it is he wants. Professor Jonathan Bracken of the drama faculty at the oldest university in the city has always known what he wants, and is certain that it is the right thing to want, despite any evidence to the contrary. How his friendship with Stella could have lasted more than thirty-five years is another story. Longevity in her nature, perhaps, like the white peony tea she favors. 壽 *sau* 眉 *mei*, "longevity's eyebrow." Visual time.

If it was a friendship.

Lately, Stella wasn't always so sure. The problem, she suspected, was his upcoming retirement at sixty, half a year away. University policy. His request this morning, awkwardly articulated in the guise of a throwaway line – *one of the smaller pieces would be nice don't you think* – a demand, really, that she should gift him one of her drawings.

In her entire life, the one thing Stella Yuen could count on was the certitude of art. Her work was acclaimed and sold extraordinarily well, although critical praise and recognition only mattered for professional longevity. What really mattered, as white hairs became inevitable, were those who had recognized and supported her art long before the art world did, who cheered her early successes, who promoted her work however they could. Her dearest friend Wai-king had died last year, and when she visited his family at home, she almost cried to see her art hanging next to the Buddhist altar table that bore his image. It had been one of her earliest pieces, long before she was *The* Stella Yuen. A later version hung at the MOMA in New York. She gifted the original sketch of that museum piece to his daughter, the girl she loved almost as if she were her own. The daughter, herself an artist, wept when she received the gift.

I ink, therefore I can be, she had told Jonathan when they first met. *You're brilliant,* he exclaimed, and kissed her on the lips right there in front of everyone at the party, drawing her so close their bodies met, making her blush violently, and for a time he was enthralled by everything she said or did or wore. They talked a lot over wine at the beginning. She told him about her mother—one of the rare persons she told, perhaps because he too was English—and he spoke of his own upbringing, difficult, not especially privileged. Hong Kong, still a colony when he first landed, had been his path to the grand life, he claimed. Despite that initial passionate outburst, Jonathan was ever the gentleman.

Late one night, several months into their friendship, he had insisted on escorting her home and had walked her up the stairs right to the door despite her protests. He invited himself in. It was the first time he saw how modestly she lived. In her tiny living room, over a nightcap, she finally told him she was a celibate. He was still jabbering nonstop as was his way, his eyes fixated on her breasts under the thin shirt when she said this—she never wore a bra and often not even panties for that matter, as she was not that night under her mini skirt, although at the time he didn't know. He stopped talking mid-phrase. *That's impossible,* he said, and then, abruptly aroused, forced his entire weight upon her on the narrow couch. Her entire physical self shrank in horror and she shoved him off. He fell to the ground, apologized profusely, and left quickly, ashamed. But for a long while afterward, years in fact, he tried to seduce her, teasing her with his roving hands whenever they were alone. *I'm not about that, don't you get it,* she repeated unfailingly, and even after he stopped trying, he kept introducing her to available men, and lesbians as well, saying, *she has higher standards than me,* until she finally ordered him *stop, please, it's offensive* and he had seemed genuinely puzzled, saying, *but I'm just teasing, I don't mean anything by it. You should know, don't you? You* know *me. Besides, you're all about visual seduction and you* know *it.*

She did know, of course she knew. All her friends called her on it and she would shrug, say, so what, I am a visual artist, aren't I? It was true she deliberately perfected a persona that belied the art that made her a memorable figure. So why should the gift of one drawing trouble her this much when she'd given away sketches and artworks to other friends, mostly those in her Chinese art world, the ones who loved that persona, encouraged it, who never let that get in the way of how they saw her as an artist? Never to him though, although she couldn't quite say why. Of course, no one else had ever come right out and *asked.* Jonathan had been a kind of supporter, showing up at all her early shows, although he never appeared to really see her work, not the way Wai-king, a professor of Chinese art history, did. And he never bought a single piece, not even back when she badly needed the money, choosing to take her out for drinks and dinners and social functions instead, introducing her to his expatriate friends who swooned over her work, wallets and checkbooks in hand. She didn't hold that against him though, not really. Art needed to be found, discovered, *felt*, not merely bought. At least, this was what she told art students in her lectures around the world, adding, *trust your art, if it is to survive, it will. Never sell yourself short.*

Meanwhile, this Abstraction in D simply wasn't happening. She slept badly that night. The next morning, instead of heading straight up to the studio as she normally would, she lay in bed and turned on her iPhone to check email. A stream from Jonathan pinged. She studiously ignored these. Scanning rapidly through the multitude of other messages, she stopped. There it was again, another e-vite from Cre-INK-eD. She was about to delete it when a text from Jonathan flashed, *good morning darling, you are up, aren't you?* Irritation rankled. Stupid, she knew, to let this get to her: it was just the way he was, but this morning, it was more than she could take, so she ignored him, opened the e-vite instead, and followed the link to their Vimeo page.

Was it perhaps another think tank, she wondered as the three-minute video ended. Lately, the global circus landed regularly on Stella's electronic doorstep. The last group, a "Sigh for Peace" initiative, had been little more than an uninspired sound art installation. What they wanted from her was a visual centerpiece—relevance be damned—and the inclusion of her name on their "worldwide collaborative art happenstance." She had declined. At last count, their video on YouTube totaled slightly under 500 views. Not nearly enough to shake up anyone's world.

This one probably wasn't much different, but at least they seemed marginally relevant to what she did.

Cre-INK-eD's e-vite first flashed into her inbox around six months prior. She had deleted it after a quick scan. Yet their message kept returning, not often enough to be annoying, but just enough to be noticed. Each message teased a little more, a slow burn, igniting desire to which she had now succumbed. Not malware, fortunately, which briefly crossed her mind.

Meanwhile, her desk beckoned.

It really was my desk, she had said to the man who did not want to sell, the man who used to run a Sheung Wan shophouse and brewed the best sour-plum tea. She had sighted the desk in the corner where his granddaughter sat doing homework. Underneath the lid, etched with her pen knife and inked violet, were His initials and the middle four digits of His phone number, her secret code. The number she never called. The violet ink had faded, but the letters and numbers were unmistakably her imprint. She had been in Form Four, the year of inking dreamily until her heart was broken by a boy who didn't care she existed. After that, she inked seriously as consolation, and here she was now, or so she told the man, having skipped the story about the boy. *I'll buy your granddaughter a new desk and an iPad.* The girl's eyes widened with desire and that sealed the deal. She never asked how he had acquired it. Didn't matter, it was hers again, as it had been now for some twenty-five years.

The schoolroom desk was her only reminder of an adolescence which had been barely tolerable. Childhood was long deleted.

Her sketch worried her. The D was derivative, which was not in and of itself the problem, except that it was derivative of herself, a '79 work. Not that anyone would know, since she had destroyed the original. But she knew. She uncapped the violet ink bottle. The pens, cleaned and gleaming as she left them each evening, sat in their holders on the wall. She removed two, one with a fine nib, the other medium, and set to work. *Today*. She would solve the problem today once and for all.

By noon, she conceded that nothing was working and considered lunch. A glance at her iPhone showed three new texts and four more emails from Jonathan. If only a sigh truly brought peace! Refusing to read these, their pattern of discourse irritatingly familiar, she conjured up noodles.

A ten-minute walk and she arrived at One Bowl of Noodles, the translation of a small eatery with only a Chinese name uphill on Star Street in what she sometimes thought of as New Wan Chai. Except that it wasn't really new. During her childhood, she and her father had lived downhill around the corner on St. Francis Yard for a brief time, when her mother still visited. Thank the stars for gentrification. It eradicated surface reality and all that should be forgotten.

The chef nodded at her in silent recognition. Stella liked

this anonymous familiarity, this lack of insistence on conversation. And the gigantic, if pricey, bowl of noodles, enough for both lunch and dinner. She ate in peace.

In the afternoon she succumbed to her inbox and reopened yesterday's e-vite. The logo, name, and slogan produced a different effect on-screen: more persistent and serious, demanding attention.

Cre-INK-eD

Creative Thinkers Ink Desire

The future is ours to see

Was the *"Que Sera Sera"* reverse echo accidental or deliberate? She wanted to believe the latter but thought the former more likely. A decade earlier, some sweet young thing had exclaimed in delight at the ICP baseball cap on her head—*oh wow, you're a fan of Insane Clown Posse too?!*—and she had to gently revise that instead to the International Center of Photography in New York from where she had acquired the black cap with its clean white lettering. Of course, thanks to that encounter, she discovered the hip-hop duo that she had not known existed.

Almost Halloween. ICP's "Night of the Chainsaw" generated over a million YouTube views. *That* was significance of a kind she didn't fully understand.

But Cre-INK-eD. She read their enigmatic invitation again, addressed to her. The email was personalized, if not truly personal, because it at least referenced her work, and was signed with a stylized I, by one Ian Hong. Who was Ian Hong? She tried searching but only turned up a bunch of LinkedIn and Facebook profiles. Countenances of hope. *Hire me. Buy my service, product, whatever. Remember me please in this galaxy of forgettables?*

Forget Ian Hong, he wasn't the problem. Jonathan was. Sighing before she could catch herself, she read through his messages chronologically. *Please,* read the latest message, a text. Sad. She rang him; he was at home, predictably, chained to his computer. *I'll be right over,* she promised. *Uncork the wine.*

In the taxi, however, that silly slogan reasserted its claim: *creative thinkers ink desire.* The untitled piece she had chosen for Jonathan, what was it really? She had never tried to exhibit it, never put it in a gallery catalogue even though her regular one had begged for it. The time she tried to pencil in a title, she wrote "Ink," but a strange flush of shame—that was the only word to describe what happened—flooded her, and she immediately erased the name. She had never told a soul. Even the memory was embarrassing.

So why, of all the random pieces in her stash, had she chosen this one for him? She tried to recall when she had first made this piece of art but couldn't be sure, except that it was a long time ago. The time she had showed it to Howard, the gallery's acquisitions manager, was accidental, because it was caught and hidden between two other pieces of art she had wanted to show. Howard had been riveted by it, exclaiming *you've never done anything like this before,* and she had to excuse herself and pretend she'd gotten a call because an overwhelming sense of—what?—assailed her and she was afraid her expression would give her away.

The taxi stopped, a welcome intrusion prodding her out of

such unnecessary remembrances.

Jonathan's flat, high up in Pokfulam overlooking the harbor's western approach, was visually boring. The interior, that is, despite its astounding view. His conservative, safe aesthetic made young local women swoon, stories of conquests he regaled her with over too many bottles of wine. His wine collection, on the other hand, was first rate, a reason, perhaps, Stella mused as she stood on his doorstep, that she tolerated their odd friendship. He had made amends after the last incident with the interior designer by sending over half a case of an excellent Oregonian Pinot Noir.

His immediate appearance on the first ring might have suggested, were she feeling unkind, that he had been pacing, hovering. He feigned surprise at how quickly she arrived, even though twenty minutes by taxi outside rush hour was no big deal. Under her arm was the long, rolled-up art.

"Darling," he kissed both cheeks but did not otherwise touch her, as they had long agreed should be their protocol. "You brought it!" And then, taking in her skinny jeans, stiletto sandals, and low-cut top that clung-hung alluringly, added, "And divine, as always."

He never called anyone darling, except her. The girls were all "angel," "sweetie," "dolly bird," or, for the especially sensual ones, "siren." *Why me*, she had finally asked around seven years earlier, and his response baffled her—*why because you're my artist of course, didn't you know?* But right now she was uneasy. Provoked. This insistence that she gift him one of her works struck her as curiously wrong, as if he measured their friendship by whether or not he received one. *To remember you by in my retirement,* he had said with a laugh when he first asked, although somehow, that had not rung quite true. Which was why she had been procrastinating.

Unrolling it, he held up what was for her a medium-sized piece. "Brilliant," he said, although he merely glanced at it before turning his gaze back towards her. He rolled it up, thanked her in his charming way, and then began pouring wine, complaining and preening all the while, and by the time she left, she wondered what their time together that evening had really been about.

In the days and weeks that followed, he no longer bothered her and she decided that this was the best thing. She had solved the problem as she set out to do, and that was that. Even her two brief glimpses at what might have been titled "Ink," the first when she pulled it out of the archives and rolled it up almost immediately, and the second when Jonathan unrolled it, no longer troubled her. She slept well for a long stretch of time, pleased that this particular problem of Jonathan had been satisfactorily laid to rest.

She was wrong, however, about Cre-INK-eD, because they turned out to be a new gallery in London, a good one, and before she knew it she was scheduled for an opening a year hence, right around Halloween.

Pleased, she called to let him know. "Jonathan, guess what," she began, and was surprised when he said, "I'll see you there then."

"What on earth do you mean?"

"In London. I'll have retired, moved back to England."

"But when?"

"Next spring." When she remained silent, still in shock over this revelation, he continued. "I don't have any choice, surely you knew? They throw you out of your university rentals here when you retire."

Surely she couldn't have known, she told herself several weeks later, as she dressed to meet him for their last supper, as he persisted in calling it. It was warm for early December, and she chose an off-the-shoulder dress, short but not too short that fit snugly, the way he liked her to dress and also because he had asked her to wear "something somewhat revealing," and wrapped herself in a large cashmere shawl. Why he wanted to take her to the W Hotel to eat, she couldn't fathom. He knew she didn't care for gourmet cuisine or luxurious surroundings, and for years had told him to take his dolly birds and sweeties who would be properly impressed. Her only weakness was fine wine, which she would happily drink with a cheap dish of dumplings. *Humor me,* he said. *One last time?*

Even though succumbing to his wishes should have tied her in a knot, since that was the pattern, tonight she felt weirdly liberated, almost wild, as if she were once again a rebellious young artist, willing to upset any and all conventions. In a reckless final moment of her toilette, she sprayed on his favorite scent, a slightly-too-cloying fragrance he had given her, back in the days before their détente, back when she still let him tease her.

But when she sat down at the table, she immediately knew something was wrong. For one thing, he was on time, early in fact, which never happened. Also, he had risen to greet her, pulling out her chair, exhibiting a chivalry that had long disappeared from their social intercourse. She dismissed her unease, accepted the delicious Sancerre, and toasted him, wishing him well in his retirement. His response—a scowl?—arrested her momentarily, but then he was Jonathan again: ostentatious, jovial, indulgent. Dinner was ordered, the first course arrived. The first bottle was already empty but Stella had only finished half of her first glass. The second bottle arrived. Jonathan was unstoppable.

Midway through their mains—Stella picked at the overpriced fish that tasted no better than one from the supermarket—Jonathan stopped eating. *I have something to say,* he declared, loud enough so that a few diners at other tables turned to stare. Stella, head bent over the dissection of her fish, looked up, startled.

He lowered his voice. *But not here. Upstairs. I have a suite booked for us.*

He did not wait for her to respond or object or anything and simply stood up, walked round to her chair and pointedly placed both hands on the back and pulled just hard enough so that she was forced to rise. A waiter appeared with her shawl, which she wrapped quickly around herself, feeling suddenly naked. Her, Stella Yuen, the artist whose presence always commanded the gaze because she was tall, striking, always dramatically and revealingly dressed, *famous.* Not vulnerable like this. Never like this. She heard the murmurs of recognition around her.

His hand grazed her bare shoulder, a blade across her skin, and circled the back of her neck. He leaned close, said, *remember when you told me about the desk,* and his hand moved down against her back, propelling her forward. Seething, she looked straight ahead, would not turn towards him. The elevator ride was silent.

Inside the suite, her eyes aflame, she stood, back against the door. "What the fuck do you…"

He was standing about a foot away, simply staring at her and began his monologue-lecture, shutting out her voice. *Did you know that your right eye is larger than your left? That you have a mole on the back of your left thigh that peeks out of your bikini bottom? Well, one-piece now, since you stopped wearing bikinis after you turned forty. Silly, I always thought. You still have the figure for it. No other woman wears a cheongsam as perfectly as you. Or high heels. You actually know how to walk in heels. Young girls today lack deportment and walk dreadfully in heels. Darling, you were always my best partner, especially when there were a lot more formal occasions for us to attend. Remember years ago the first time you stripped for me, when we sailed out beyond Sai Kung to a private cove, just the two of us. When we were young and too horny? I came, had to leap into the water so you wouldn't know. It was embarrassing.*

"Why are you telling me all this?"

Turn around, don't look at me. I've led a lousy life. You were the one true thing in my entire time here.

She continued to glare at him.

The desk, the time you told me about the desk and how that boy you had such a mad crush on made fun of you, humiliated you by saying to everyone at the party where he danced with you that you weren't wearing a bra? After that was when you started nude

modeling and when your father found out he called you a disgrace.
I tried to comfort you, held you, told you to cry but you refused.

He moved towards an ice bucket where a bottle of champagne rested, and popped the cork. Handing her an overflowing flute, he placed his hand on her hip. *Come on, just once.*
Once, that's all. I've been waiting almost a lifetime. We belong to each other—you know that, don't you? He stepped back, poured himself a glass and came towards her again. *Please?* This time his hand moved over her bared skin, sliding down along the snug fit of her skirt, the smooth snugness her skin. She did not remove his hand the sensation was so foreign. *Almost a lifetime,* he repeated, his teeth against her earlobe.

In the morning, he was gone before her. A note on his pillow said, *everything's taken care of, you can just drop off the key at reception.* It was as if she had dreamed it all. She did not see Jonathan again in Hong Kong, and then, she received a message from him with his new contact information in, of all places, Mole Valley, England.

In fall the following year, right around Halloween as a matter of fact, she was sipping wine at her opening. Stella was glad to be away from Hong Kong, even though autumn was the best time of year, because even that season had become impossible for taking deep, long breaths. She didn't like to complain about pollution—too clichéd—but the truth was less original than anyone would admit. London was crisper, more invigorating, a clear-headed jolt.

Jonathan was at her opening, his hair darker than it had been, with some younger English rose on his arm and looked good, as Stella told him he did.

"Thanks to you, darling," he replied, gesturing towards the young woman in a manner that suggested *run along now dear, this is a serious conversation for grownups.* The woman made a beeline for the drinks table, swaying on stilettoes.

What did he mean, she wondered, what was he talking about, but another artist floated by with an interested buyer, distracting her during this headily successful opening.

It was not till sometime later that evening that she saw him again. He was in a corner, buzzed. The English rose was nowhere in sight.

He tilted his head, stared at her and did not say anything. Disconcerting. She wondered if he were drunker than he appeared. "Jonathan? Are you okay?"

"I'm fine," he said. "How's Hong Kong? How's the studio in Wan Chai?"

"Still there."

He took her hand, held onto it. "Do you remember the first time you invited me up? After that opening? I fell asleep on the lounge chair outside and when I awoke, I could see stars, while below the city thrummed on into the night."

A strangely nostalgic tone! It was unlike him. She said. "A long time ago. So do you like being back in England?"

"No."

His abrupt anger startled her. "I never pictured you in rural life."

He turned and gazed briefly around the room. "Neither did I. Anyway, another successful show, darling," and turned back to face her. "But then, you always are successful, aren't you?"

His expression was jagged and his tone bitter, almost hostile. He clutched her hand so tightly she wanted to say, *stop, please.* As hard as she tried to dismiss her reaction—*an overreaction, surely she was mistaken*—she couldn't. "Well," she said, trying to smile, "you haven't done so badly yourself?"

He stared hard at her. "When do you go back?"

She looked away. "Tomorrow evening."

"Must feel nice to be able to go home."

"You too, surely?" Now, she tried to remove her hand from his but he hung onto it, almost unaware he was doing so.

"To Mole Valley? You're joking, of course." Then, after a pause. "Thank you."

"For what?"

"Why, your drawing, of course," he began, slowly, deliberately. "It gave me a ho... a pensioner's cottage."

What he said did not immediately hit home, but when it did, seconds later, she stared at him in horror.

You, she began, but couldn't complete the sentence.

"Yes," he continued, his old self again, "the Chinese buyer was delighted that it had a personal message from you on the back. I told him you did it especially for him."

You never said, she began, but he had released her hand and was already kissing her goodbye, saying "darling so good to see you and congratulations again come for drinks and dinner next time you're in London," and handed her his card.

Ian Hong waltzed by right then. "This has been brilliant, thank you, thank you so very much again, Ms. Yuen," and whirled her away, and then she was surrounded once more by her public and world till the night ended.

That night, she awoke around three, drenched in sweat, wet between her legs. The night with Jonathan at the W suite returned full force, their bodies entwined as they fucked as if survival depended on it. Afterward, she had lain on her back and stared at the ceiling that looked askew. *Ink*, she had said. *That's what it's called and I made it for you after that night when I told you about the desk. I made it for you.* But he had fallen asleep and then she drifted off and only their bodies carried the imprint of all they had been.

Afterward, when she was safely back home and the shock had abated, she turned the problem over and over again in her mind, unable to make sense of it. Jonathan wasn't rich, but a professor at the University of Hong Kong made more money than many management executives in the UK. He certainly must at least be comfortable. Or was he? His flat in Hong Kong was rented, which might be why retirement seemed so difficult for him. But she assumed, had always assumed, that he had invested in a flat in Hong Kong, renting it out until time for retirement arrived. She never once imagined he would leave Hong Kong. It was what everyone else did, surely, if they didn't have a home somewhere as Jonathan clearly didn't in England. However, his indulgences in travel, food, wine, women were extravagant; she sometimes wondered how he afforded it all but assumed he managed. Had she missed all signs of who he really was? Had she never really known him at all?

Was *that* the problem?

The days dragged. All she could think about was Jonathan until the afternoon she sat at One Bowl of Noodles, unable to swallow a single bite of her meal, igniting a slow burn. She finally called him in the evening, and he was surprised at her angry outburst. It never occurred to him that the gift was personal, he said, or that to sell it meant such a great betrayal. *None of my friends would dream of doing such a thing,* she told him. He remained unfazed. He honestly did not understand what she was so upset about and then he changed the subject, as he was so good at doing, and refused to discuss the matter any further.

OFF THE RECORD

for Jason Wordie

What I am going to say is old stuff with which you are all familiar. There is nothing new
... There are still things in this revolution which have not been completed and must still be continued: for example struggle-criticism-transformation. After a few years maybe we shall have to carry out another revolution.

Chairman Mao: Speech at the first plenum of the CCP, April 28, 1969

THE **first time they kissed, their mouths locked for thirty-five seconds before she broke off and said, this will be off the record of course?** He had been surprised at the question, because he already presumed it, but with Frieda Andersson, he would never be quite sure of anything. Their affair had begun in his youth – an odd notion, youth – and almost forty years later he wondered why it was that of all the women he had known, Frieda was the only one who lingered, viscerally, the coffee flavor of her tongue as instant as if she were still alive, breathing against his neck. This one, quick, perpetually unattainable.

This morning, he was anticipating his trip to Athens and the side trip to Hydra. He did not really need to go to Greece. The last time there had been when he'd first met Frieda on the island of Hydra, during the years he was living in that country. Well, twenty-two months really, hardly years, and not continuously as he'd done so on a tourist visa, requiring exits and re-entries, which did not exactly constitute "residence," unlike Frieda who previously really was resident in Athens as an employee of an American research institute, although when they met she was living in Hong Kong and worked for the U.S. Consulate.

His PA called. The upgrade to a premium seat on Turkish had come through. It would only be his second time flying that airline and he relished it, fed up as he was with Cathay Pacific. Besides, the threat of a pilots' work-to-rule action loomed, and that meant delays. No, Turkish was fine. It was Star Alliance so he'd get mileage points, and these days, points meant life still embraced travel, and travel, these days, was a necessary reprieve from home.

His PA. A pretty young thing. She had been his PA for almost nine months. Very young, but anyone under forty-five felt very young now. When had that tipping point occurred, when younger equated off limits, even for friendship, never mind anything else? *Why forty-five,* his best friend Mark had asked a fortnight prior when they met for drinks and food. He had no real answer. Arbitrary, he supposed, although what he wouldn't confess to was a profound lack of interest in sex, despite a functional libido, certainly healthier than Mark's— he popped Viagra—and whose American wife of a lifetime was caught up in an affair with a younger man, a hotshot at the investment bank from which Mark was now retired.

He worked till his stomach beckoned lunch. The piece for *GoAsia* was due today. Easy, churning out travel writing for younger editors who were always frenzied, undisciplined, and seldom rigorous. Once upon a time he had been a real news journalist for hawk-eyed editors, but that life was over now, as perhaps was real journalism. At least for Asian media. You couldn't report the news when everything was sanitized along the sightlines of a region in awe of China. You *especially* couldn't do it in Chinese, which he had long ago abandoned in favor of English-language bylines, the advantage of his true bilingual ability. Which was what had been attractive about Frieda, who spoke both Mandarin *and* Cantonese with native-like fluency and was highly literate. And she wasn't even part Chinese, like he, or his PA, who spoke fluently but was barely literate, having gone through international schools locally and was now quite Anglicized after uni in England.

Why do you need a PA, Mark also asked. That was easy, for the contract work which he mostly did write in Chinese. In the last fifteen or so years, he made a lucrative living as a ghostwriter of commissioned autobiographies for the rich and pompous. Business tycoons, newly-rich society wannabes, retired civil servants, philanthropists, scientists, doctors, and other members of the elite, even a few Hong Kong Chinese academics who, despite an international intellectual life presumably well lived, could not articulate deeper thoughts in elegant Chinese without assistance. Asia, China in particular, was good for all that, which was why he remained in Hong

Kong, even though the crowds and pollution daily irritated. There seemed to be an endless supply of clients who would pay for a gorgeously manufactured volume of their lives and musings for their heirs and other toadies. Which was why he needed a PA swan. Sherry swanned brilliantly, effortlessly sipping champagne and *mao tai* around such potentials—mostly men, a few society ladies, those wives with easy access to their husband's fortune—her clever tongue constantly at work in English, French, and three Chinese dialects, her PR training and natural charm all grand assets. Sherry was maybe thirty-five, tall enough to be seriously present, exotic enough to be sexy, blessed with a Hello Kitty demeanor that seduced but did not intimidate. Sherry was more intelligent than she looked, and financially married so did not need to earn much. He was just famous enough to warrant her attention.

Sherry called again. Another potential job, a society wife, *although you might like this one,* she added. *She's not a twit.* His pulse quickened when she said who it was. A good PA who knew him, sometimes even more than he preferred. The appointment was for later that afternoon, tea at the Landmark. Why anyone took tea in an echo chamber atrium of this shopping mall and office tower he never understood, but who was he to question fashion?

Liana Hung Jordan was dressed for attention. They arrived at the same moment, and he introduced himself while she once-over'ed him, her lips a sly smirk. He was dressed, as usual, in jeans and a tailored white shirt.

"You're not quite what I expected," she said after their

orders were given, she an obvious regular. The captain had personally looked after them. "I thought you'd be..."

"More bohemian?"

"Older."

She was in her early thirties, and her divorce last year from Brent Jordan had made global society news, given the gargantuan settlement. Jordan was the British billionaire from South Africa, owner of the executive jet company CatMouse Air, a producer of blockbuster martial arts movies, the patron saint of art museums to which he regularly loaned his extensive collection of contemporary Chinese art, and, most recently, the man who founded *WorldChina 21*, bilingually published online and reputed to be paying *unbelievably* generous salaries to young and even not-so-young journalists who signed on full-time and agreed to dwell in the "heart" of China. *Xanadu,* Jordan declared at the press conference to unveil his latest enterprise, *WorldChina 21 is all about Xanadu in the 21ˢᵗ Century.*

"Are you disappointed?"

"No." She drew out the "o," rounding her lips as if sucking on a straw. "Pleased, actually. I know your reputation and am delighted that being distinguished doesn't equal old and fat."

No one had ever called him "distinguished" before. Her ex was at least fifteen years his junior and as obese as a Roman emperor could become and still rule.

He said, "So what can I do for you?"

She unbuttoned her pale pink angora sweater to reveal a white designer T and low neckline. His quick glance took in a subtly bared midriff. "Oh, so right down to business, are we?" Her accent was vaguely British.

Afterward, he was furious at his imagination, a riotous, unstoppable movie reel of Liana in every position known to porn.

Sherry was as surprised as he that Liana Hung Jordan did not want a ghostwriter. Instead, she wanted him to interview her for a book by him in English. He'd told Liana he had to think about this and that Sherry would be in touch. She had actually said, *I'll make it worth your while,* and then picked the cherry off her cake and, eyes widened, stuck her tongue out and popped it whole into her mouth. The woman was boringly vulgar, although marrying Brent Jordan should have been sufficient evidence of that.

So you'll do it? The anxiety in Sherry's voice was palpable.

He couldn't, of course he wouldn't. He *knew* he couldn't. Liana had also actually said, *I want to outsell Monica Lewinsky,* as if that were the measure of a life. Of course, she still had a lot of life left and perhaps could be forgiven for seeing this as simply another project for a society gal's perpetual-motion machine that passed for living. Eliana Hung was local, the only daughter of a former Chinese-American diplomat and Portuguese mother; her father left his first career, hunkered down in Hong Kong where he made a fortune as a property tycoon, and her mother sent her off to a French lycée and Swiss finishing school; the family staged their own private version of a debutante's ball for her in London, where she met her ex—his family was listed in Debrett's—before he was fat and fucking Thai prostitutes.

Yet what he told Sherry was *I'll think on it and tell you after my trip?* He heard the quick, sharp breath over the phone, a sign his PA was worried. He recalled—Sherry and Liana had been in school together as girls, how had she put it, *not the same circles but we weren't unfriendly*—and now, Eliana (Liana) Hung Jordan (she did not drop her married name) called a lot of shots in the global playground that mattered to Sherry.

To reassure, he reminded her that there should be no rush, this being just over two weeks before Christmas and the season a whirl of parties so surely his decision could wait till the new year, mid-January, after his return from Athens? *Tell her that*, and added, *oh, and have a good Christmas.*

Later, he decided to check out the last night of Occupy in Admiralty. The tents lined the closed highway and he remained on the overpass to gaze at the students and other protestors below. Diehards. Even if he had returned to Hong Kong unwillingly to minister to his dying father—an inoperable brain tumor, excruciating pain numbed by morphine—at least he was witness to this one, truly fine moment of his birthplace, this city he no longer loved, the city which had disappointed him for too long now, a city which was only good for making more money than he could make anywhere else in the world to ensure his more-or-less estranged father could die with some dignity.

Years ago, he had escaped to Greece with no intention of returning, or so he thought at the time. Northwestern and Medill for his master's in journalism followed, as did jobs in Chicago and London, but in the nineties, his mother had begged him to come home when jobs for someone like him were plentiful. He had never been able to say no to

Ma. Besides, those years at *The Wall Street Journal Asia* had been something, his last moment as a real journalist, when his features made the front page middle column on a regular basis. Ma died before the millennium and there was no one to care for his father, this exiled-by-choice-and-tax-avoidance American. His only sister, older, had run away years earlier and now had a real family and grandchildren in Melbourne. They rarely communicated. Which left him. *Promise me*, Ma said, her sense of melodrama and compassion intact on her deathbed, *you'll take care of him?* And so he did.

It's not so bad here, Mark said. *At least the public transport and food's good.* They had been boys together at KGV, King George the Fifth, one of the few Anglo schools in a colonial age when being half Chinese was still odd. Not so now. The more things changed, the more people evolved in this city where things, meanwhile, remained the same. The elite that dominated property and society. White Anglo privilege. A Cantonese mafia that governed, these 21st century running dogs to the Party in Beijing. Had it been a blessing or curse that Ma made him more Chinese than he felt? She taught Chinese literature and history at one of the universities, and if she couldn't tame her daughter into cultural and linguistic submission, she ensured her son would inherit and nurture her earth.

As he walked Occupy now, copy ran through his head, like a teletype news ticker of the almost obsolete newspaper world in his blood. You can't live without blood, just as he couldn't live without some connection to the written word, even if what he wrote these days paled against what had once made him thrive. *It's still writing,* Mark said, *and we're still alive and sort of kicking.* And *I can still afford to buy you dinner at the Hong Kong Club.* Old friends made a difference, and Mark's family had been a refuge in the face of his father's irrational violence. How had Ma tolerated him so long? The reporting that won him his Pulitzer was on domestic violence in Chicago from where his father hailed.

Frieda told him secrets of violent men in the diplomatic corps: *tiger brains,* she called them. *Vicious. Barely human.*

He stopped at a wall of post-its on the barricaded stairway at the northern end of the overpass and snapped a photo on his cell. He wasn't sure why he did that. It wasn't as if he posted on Facebook or Twitter or was trying to write about Occupy. He didn't even like photos and kept few of his own life. But this written record by hundreds of people moved him. Words and swordplay. All to be cleared away later that night by the protestors before the police came to disperse them the next day.

In the morning he awoke with an erection so hard he could have been a teenager again. Damn Liana. And the scotch. Not bad for sixty-two, although what lurked as he relieved himself was Frieda, the only redhead. *Then I'll be memorable,* she had declared when he disclosed that, six months into their relationship. *Had* it been a relationship? It was prolonged but sporadic. She told him little about her background, and, when pressed, after more than a decade of intermittence, during one of their longer, two-week couplings, said she hailed from *one of those Illinois towns with funny names, you know, Paris, Oblong, Normal?* After she died, during one of those numerous

late-night drinks parties that were *de rigeur* at Mark's back in the mid-nineties, Mark's wife told him that was a line from a short story by Lorrie Moore. Even now, Frieda was still the only redhead.

He sipped coffee and listened to the radio's morning current-affairs program. Some caller complained about foreign influence, saying America should stay out of China's internal affairs, meaning both Hong Kong and Taiwan. He imagined Frieda surveying Occupy. What would she have said? For about ten months before she died, they had been in a real relationship, he a real journalist, she the deputy consul general of Hong Kong's U.S. Consulate, both resident in the same city at the same time. They came to each other late at night, after hours, *off the record* she reminded him, usually after sex. Yet whenever he recollected their intense, private, sensual Eden— even Mark didn't know till a year after her death—it felt incomplete, and he thought it merely an affair, even though they both were unattached, even though each one sidestepped any other serious relationship. *We can't be public,* she insisted. *Our careers are conflicted interests.* He offered to quit since newsprint was quickly evaporating. Even back then, people approached him about vanity book deals, mostly profiles for successful Chinese businessmen. *Don't,* she said. *Don't compromise yourself* just *for this.*

On the radio news, the U.S. Consulate's spokesman denied any American government involvement in Occupy.

An unfamiliar number beamed from his cellphone. Thinking it might be the airline, he answered.

"What's your ringtone for unknown callers?" Liana's voice held an edge.

"I don't have one. What can I do for you?"

"So you're really going to make me wait till January? Look, pop by for drinks tonight and we'll discuss this some more. Maybe I need to, ah, convince you?"

The woman was as transparent as Frieda had been opaque. He half expected her to ask him to guess what she *wasn't* wearing.

"Can't, sorry," and he excused himself with his upcoming trip, saying there was simply too much to do.

"I *adore* Greece! Where will you be? We could meet up there."

He should say no, now, right now, and he knew it. But she pulled an "so sorry must run listen don't go away without seeing me please?" and was gone. His first thought was to call Sherry. Visions of Liana, like some obscene sugar-plum fairy, stopped him. This would not do, this simply would not do. He would not end up in bed with that woman. He regretted having been polite, and charming, having listened sympathetically to her story over tea until she was ready to fuck him. His bad, the way he seduced women, even the ones he didn't want to sleep with. A habit to break. Since Frieda, a habit to console his wounded heart, to fill the unbearable absence caused by the only woman he had ever been able to love.

So what was this libido resurrection? Liana as consolation prize?

Mark had declared, ten years after Frieda died, *she must have been a spy.* His response, a tongue-lashing delivered with venomous ferocity, shocked even him. For several months, Mark and he kept their distance. He hadn't told Mark much about the way things had been. Being with Frieda was exciting, sexy, romantic, and the secrecy jazzed him. It had also been easier when he still lived in Chicago, and later London, when she fed him stories that made editors salivate, this unnamed source he protected. She did seem to know a lot about U.S. foreign policy, and everything she told him eventually turned out to be true. They met in Berlin, Geneva, New York, anywhere. He took her to Key West where they fucked till dawn. The year before Tiananmen, she was posted to Beijing and they walked along the Great Wall together, staring at the vastness before them, far from any madding crowds, before China's prosperity had transformed the nation into its crowd-sourced, mad consumption. If they met in her city of residence, which was seldom, they did so publicly, around other people, he the visiting friend for general consumption. Their trysts were confined to a third location, away from his hotel or her apartment. He could have loved her forever like this, no family or friends involved. Once, an associate of hers mentioned an ex-husband *or maybe not quite ex*, she added. He didn't pay much attention, since the woman had made a play for him and was being catty. Besides he felt he knew enough of Frieda's professional world to believe the real parts of her story: Chinese studies at Yale; a long-ish stint as a grad student in Taiwan to perfect the language; a briefer stint with USAID in Thailand; some Greek blood. Once, she had shown him a snapshot of parents, both dead, she said. They looked like her. She claimed to be an only child.

He had a meeting in Central late that afternoon and the taxi from his home in Wan Chai sailed through the emptied thoroughfare that only yesterday housed a tented district, closed to all traffic. *Thank heavens they're gone*, the driver said. *More than two months! Youth. Such a nuisance, eh?* To the north, the waterfront flashed by. The Ferris wheel popped in and out of view.

In the middle of his meeting with an Asia travel guidebook series editor, his text message box pinged three times in rapid succession. He glimpsed the teardrop on a sad face ending the last message. The editor caught sight of it on his screen and smiled. *Woman problems, eh*, he remarked. He turned his phone over, embarrassed, and laughed it off. As he was walking out of the meeting Mark called, wanting to meet for drinks, *but in the hole not the club*. Something had to be amiss, so he said yes of course, and agreed to half eight. Meanwhile the problem of Liana—who else would send those ridiculous texts—and sure enough, there they were, all cutesy and pouty, like some teenage princess, except that this was a grown woman with more money than sense and too much time to burn.

He tried to call Sherry but she wasn't answering. That hardly ever happened because his PA was glued to her phone and usually answered on the first ring, or else it rolled over to voicemail that said she was on another line. Now, it rang and rang. Perhaps she'd left already but no, he was positive she wasn't flying out to Burma on holiday with her husband for at least another week. He tried calling again. No luck. He finally gave up, thought briefly about texting or emailing but decided against it. He should talk to Sherry, explain how impossible Liana would be for him to work with, and ask her to decline as diplomatically as he knew she could.

He stopped at the corner of Ice House and Chater, trying to decide what to do next. At this hour, the MTR would be unbearably crowded. The ferry made more sense. He was about to cross the road to head to the pier when an arm slid through the crook of his and there she was, in a absurdly snug, too-short skirt and a pair of Jimmy Choo's stilettoes. Shit. Now what?

"You're avoiding me, aren't you?"

Her eyes were too bright and she was standing precariously close to the edge of the sidewalk.

"Oh, hello," he said and disentangled his arm. "What a coincidence."

"Yesterday you were almost tearing my clothes off with your eyes and then you desert me. What's that all about?" Her voice was too loud and people were staring. "Are you a cunt tease? Is that it? It's not very nice, you know."

She clutched at her long, loose, bright green sweater that was sliding off one arm towards the ground. He reached to pull the sleeve up but her arm flailed, barring his. "Don't touch me!" She was almost shouting now. "You men are all the same."

If he dared, he would have just walked away, but she was clearly disturbed, or high, or something, and in need of assistance. He glanced down the road. Surely a car and driver would appear any minute now and whisk her away? At least he hoped it would, before anyone he knew came by and witnessed this bizarre tableau. It was just past seven, and the streets teemed with office workers headed off into their evenings. Liana turned away from him and doubled over, as if in pain, and for a moment, he was afraid she might collapse onto the ground. Then, a younger Chinese woman appeared, calling her name. She straightened up, waved and smiled, and the two of them took off together.

He watched her go, more puzzled than annoyed. Liana didn't even turn around to acknowledge him. It was as if he had never existed. What was she playing at? Why was she being so persistent? He did not flatter himself into believing that his seduction had really been all that successful. Besides, she could have any man she wanted, and regularly did, if the gossip was to be believed. The other woman was less hooker-chic than Liana, but she looked moneyed too, another society girl.

A redhead crossed his line of sight, headed for the taxi stand on Chater. Tall, fair, long-limbed. He had to stop himself from going up to her to say, *Frieda Andersson, how nice to see you,* the way he used to whenever they accidentally-on-purpose ran into each other, when she couldn't come to him for a late-night tryst, when he had to content himself with seeing her somewhere for a few minutes of conversation while they fucked each other with their eyes, in view of the world. It was a game they played, and this, he realized, was what made Liana so irritatingly present in his imagination. She had Frieda's long-limbed build, but was far more crudely irresistible, fuckable, and she was playing him too, the way Frieda had.

He stepped out on the road, only to be blared at by a taxi. Rattled, he jumped back onto the curb.

Dangerous daydreaming, Mark would say to him, much later that night at the hole, his words slurred. *You always were a dreamer.*

The hole, a bar in Tsim Sha Tsui they met at when they didn't want to run into anyone they knew, was at the intersection of two short side streets. One was a lane that didn't show up on Google maps. They had discovered it as teenagers and, despite several management changes over the years, it basically remained a dive bar. Back in their schooldays, during Vietnam, it had been frequented by American sailors on shore leave who got into fights with British army blokes until the MPs broke things up. The mama-san used to tell them to go home, to get the hell out of this hole. But she liked them both, gave them free beers and food. Mark especially made her laugh, this *bak gwaijaai,* a pale, blond boy who swore in pitch-perfect Cantonese, who hung with his *jaap jung* friend, a boy who could have been one of her own girls' mixed-race kids by their vanished johns. *No money no honey.* Today the bar was glitzier, spruced up, but still a hole, for transients and mainland tourists who contributed to the high occupancy of the numerous small hotels that had sprung up in recent years. Even this district, Tsim Sha Tsui, had transformed from "Tsimsy" of their colonial past into TST. The more the city changed, the more he wanted out of this hellish swamp that only had Mark as an anchor.

Mark looked like hell warmed over, which was what he said when he arrived a little after eight. His friend was early, and looked to be already in his cups.

He asked. "What's with you?"

She's leaving me, Mark told him, and launched into a long monologue that alternated between a diatribe and lament for his about-to-become-ex wife. What could he say? It would have been their 30th anniversary next year. Their boys were grown, the older almost married in Singapore, the younger *finally* out of uni in England with his PhD in modern Chinese history, well bred, well educated, raised to survive their British-Chinese world with sufficient privilege. He had a sudden vision of Mark's younger son as a boy. Colin, the dreamy one. Curled up at home with *The Decline and Fall of the Roman Empire* when he was maybe twelve. He had come for dinner—sometime in the '80s—the evening Mark's wife was trying to set him up with a divorced English girlfriend, an attractive blonde not unlike herself. He had dropped her off afterward and headed back to his hotel room alone, where Frieda was waiting, in transit from somewhere to somewhere else, and flown back home to London a few days later.

Around two a.m., he took Mark home, made the taxi wait while he brought him up to his flat and into the bedroom. He left him lying there, mostly on his bed. His friend needed to lose some weight because it was a strain to lift him. Mark's wife was at her lover's, he'd been told, so he was startled to see her, this ghostly figure in the shadows as he made his way out. *Thanks,* she said, *I was kinda worried.* He mumbled something, conscious of his own unsteady gait, and returned to the waiting taxi and home.

He had been semi-conscious for about an hour or so when his phone rang. He answered, thinking, *his father,* but then her slurred voice grated. What did he have to do? Report her for stalking? No one would take that seriously here. He hung up without replying and switched off the ringer. His phone buzzed several more times before she finally gave up.

He did not manage to reach Sherry the next day. Meanwhile, he ignored Liana's voicemails, texts, emails that grew increasingly more agitated and accusatory. She bandied the R word. Perhaps he should be worried, but it all was too ridiculous to take seriously, and when the nurse called, one of the two he employed to provide 24-7 home care for his father, saying she had just called 999, Liana vanished from his imagining. The next day, when he was by his father's hospital bedside, after the doctor said it would be a matter of days, a week at most, Sherry called to say that Liana was dead, suicide, most likely an overdose. Heroin, he guessed. *I wanted to let you know before the media gets the information out there. Your number is probably all over her cell, as is mine.*

The next morning, Liana was all over the news. Her cellphone was not found anywhere in her home.

No one had told him about Frieda. He was away when she was found dead in her apartment, the door locked and bolted from the inside. He eventually heard it was a heart attack—these were harder to detect in women, he learned from later research—but he found it hard to believe. This was before Google, before Facebook: all paths to track down someone whose existence mattered to you were hindered by distance and the absence of electronic ease. But he was a journalist with investigative experience! Regardless, every trail he picked up and followed led to a dead end. Each odd-named small town in Illinois did not reveal an Andersson family of any kind that might have been hers. Someone at the consulate later said it was so sad about Frieda, how she had no family and all; and when he heard that, some part of his insides were wrung out dry, a fatal ambush. There wasn't even a grave somewhere to visit, an urn of ashes to hold onto. Not even a photo. It wasn't possible that this woman, who was up until only a short while ago the one intimate he counted on in the whole entire world, had now completely disappeared as if she never existed

Liana, on the other hand, should never have entered his space. In the days and weeks after her death, his anxiety lessened with each new utterance that passed as news, of reflective regret from her multitude of "friends" on social media, of electronic fashions, foods, and flowers offered up in her memory. It was like the paper replicas that once were offered for the dead by burning but now existed only *in an environmentally conscious virtuality*, as the tagline for www.GiftsforHappyGhosts.com read. Her celebrity filled the space previously occupied by the student protestors and gave his city another story for speculation until the next big thing usurped it. For the people of Hong Kong, it was far more compelling than the corrupt, extravagant former government official on trial or the utterances of Presidents Obama and Xi, since what either said didn't really matter, not really, not for their day-to-day. And they were even deafer to the mutterings of the British PM, his joint-declaration knights-errant barred from the city by its sovereign ruler, their ears more attuned to the Australian one, since at least the hostage crisis in a café right in the center of Sydney was something real, something that could happen in their own city. Many speculated on which cafés in Central made the best targets: the ones closest to the banks, they said. Governments came and went, but people carried on, surviving as best they could, thriving when the heavens smiled upon them, weeping when tragedy befell.

Sherry, shaken by the whole Liana incident, gave notice the following week. She could not, she said, continue as his PA after this, as she felt *guilty, even though it wasn't really my fault. I didn't really have anything to do with this, she was just a very troubled person, wasn't she?* Also, she was pregnant—the reason she hadn't answered her cell that day because she had *literally* just found out—and her husband and she agreed it was best if she didn't work.

In the new year, what would surprise him most was that Mark would get to keep the family flat, *for the boys*, his wife said. She didn't want divorce, it turned out, wanting only separation, and her lover, he presumed. Mark proved sanguine. He went to the gym, lost weight, and by mid-year begin dating a bevy of younger women who liked to play, no strings attached.

But right now, over coffee, on this sunny Saturday morning—ten days after the last night of Occupy in Admiralty, nine after his drink with Mark, a week after Liana's suicide, days after Sherry gave notice, and the morning after his father's demise—what thrummed through his entire being was not Frieda, not Mark, *mercifully* not Liana, and definitely not his father. Instead, what he recalled was an April day in 1969 and his mother saying at dinner, *yesterday the Chairman told the Party to stop squabbling.* He was seventeen and it made him laugh, the idea of the CCP being told off, like a bunch of naughty school kids, by their leader. That July, super-typhoon Viola made landfall in Guangdong and not Hong Kong, killing something like a thousand people, unlike typhoon Viola five years earlier that hit the city dead center and was welcome relief after a long drought. It had been hellish, filling buckets of water when rationing was just four hours a day. In 1969, there was also another Viola often on his mind, the girl he was crushing on—when did crush become a verb even he used?—the one who played gorgeous piano and had a concert career in her future. She did for a while but died young, around maybe forty. Of liver cancer, just like Ma.

And this morning, what he also remembered was the slogan Mao quoted that April day when he had scolded the party: *First, do not fear hardship; second, do not fear death.* He scanned his bookshelf and found the text of the speech, delivered at the first plenum of the Ninth Central Committee.

The Cultural Revolution would not end for another five years, but it was evident from the speech, as he read it again now, that Mao understood the nation had serious problems, even though he could not resolve them before his death. What followed the line about hardship and death struck a chord: the Chairman said that many had died, and that *the old comrades who remain are fortunate to be alive and have survived by chance.* Which was his way of saying, shut up and quit complaining, there's still life to be lived, work to be done, and that's what you should be doing. Not entirely unlike the Hong Kong government today as they chided the student protestors, although they couldn't say, not really, what needed to be done or what should happen next.

The sudden temperature drop and chilly damp of the last couple of days were giving way to a surge of warmth. The sun shone. His inbox was full but not bursting. There was a job to complete soon and today he would track down the last contact he needed. Some stories you finished, others remained forever untold, while others continued, unresolved, in perpetual anticipation. His life as a journalist, now over, these life stories he told instead, all these years of words and more words were what he could count on for this life he'd made for himself, regardless of parents, friends, Frieda. Or a Liana. He thought about Mark and hoped his friend would pull through.

He would also have to call Turkish himself and cancel his trip. It would be hellish till he found a new PA.

He finished his coffee; the taste of Frieda was his forever. History proved the Chairman wrong, spectacularly wrong about so many things. But that one time, at the start of another new moment in China, he might have been right. Familiar old stuff was just that, old, and being alive, having survived, was way better than being dead.

body & blood

CANINE NEWS

from across the Pacific or Atlantic, depending on your race, nation, language, class, cyberspace, point of view, and concept of the universal

THESE two essays recently came into our possession. *They were handwritten in a notebook. The person who sent the notebook found it on a bench along the Tsim Sha Tsui[1] promenade by the harbor. He began to read and was struck by both the extremely fine penmanship and its odd voice. A meditation on pet care, he described it, coupled with what he called a definitive Hong Kong story (we are not sure we quite agree). He asked us to see what we thought, because he believed the work should be published in our journal. We read and agreed. Only the first few pages were filled, and the rest of the notebook was blank. No name, no contact information.*

Although the person who found this notebook wishes to remain anonymous, he did ask us to publish his Twitter handle—@literatehound—for anyone wishing to follow his tweets. As the editors of this journal follow no one's tweets, we neither gain nor lose by publicizing such information, which strikes us as editorially fluid. Please do also note that until this Twitterer made contact with us, we had no previous acquaintance with him. We

1 Also rendered Tsimshatsui, or in its original form, 尖沙嘴, meaning pointed sand mouth, a district in Kowloon (or 九龍), Hong Kong (or 香港), and is basically unpronounceable in any romanization which is why non-Cantonese speakers now refer to it as TST.

still have not met him in person as he finds the journey to our offices a tad too arduous, being inclined to seasickness, although we did meet him on Skype and therefore know he exists. He was however wearing a basset hound mask when we spoke.

If the writer of these essays will make her or himself known to us, we will gladly pay a modest fee for this contribution to our journal, in any currency except the Euro which may not last beyond this century. Copyright remains with the unknown writer, although we cannot guarantee that the work will not be translated and siphoned off across borders to where international copyright laws might hold less sway. However, that is any writer's problem for losing a notebook in the first place, and especially so in Hong Kong, Special Administrative Region (also, S.A.R.) *of the People's Republic of China.*

From the Preface by the Editors

The Journal of Deficit, Disquiet & Disbelief, Vol. 13, No. 4, Senkaku, 2015

www.j-dd&d/mydao.net[2] • email: j-dd&dkitty88@mydao.net
*

---

2 DAO could be construed as pinyin for 島 meaning "island" although this is uncertain because DAO could also be pinyin for several other homonyms, including the ancient Chinese Taoist philosophy of the "way" (道) or an English acronym for the Diseases of Aquatic Organisms, a journal now up to volume 79 for which subscriptions are sold in Euros.

Anon.
In the Doghouse

I share a rooftop with a dog named Chocolate. A wall divides our space, heightened by a wire mesh fence my neighbor constructed when his family moved in. A good thing, this metal barrier, because Chocolate sometimes clings frantically to it and barks when I return home. But that's only if he's banished to his doghouse on the roof, instead of snuggled downstairs at home with his parents and sisters, the two girls who love and ignore their dog because their father takes him on nightly walks, scooping up poop, thus freeing them to indulge in their own lives, without responsibility for comprehensive pet care.

Recently, my brother in Ohio emailed an image of a beagle, prone on its doghouse rooftop. The caption read, *I always knew Snoopy was real.*

I am in the doghouse next door to Chocolate because I too am in exile. Downstairs in the flat, my mother shuffles through her deteriorating-Alzheimer's days and nights in the company of three Filipinos: two live-in domestic helpers and one nurse. Our family is lucky to have this roof room, such as it is; otherwise, I could not live "at home" with Mum, sharing the same 12th floor address, and therefore be able to legally employ the three women my mother thinks she employs (whenever she remembers to be "in charge" of her household, that is, the way she once was).

The other day, my sister who lives with her beagle on a beach over on the south side of the island said, *I must build Beagle a doghouse.* My sister likes precision in nomenclature, although it makes me wonder why my nephew's name isn't either Son or Male.

The Faces of Beagle

This morning, the *South China Morning Post* ran the headline, *We love our neighbours, but only if they're like us.*[3]

Apparently, Hongkongers ranked highest in a world survey for the percentage of respondents who selected "people of a different race" when asked who they would not want as neighbors. This is no surprise. I do not like sharing a rooftop with a discontented mutt, in exile, whenever the humans below want to be home alone with their own kind. Of course, I'm not certain if Chocolate is in fact of a different race. His name is reasonably precise, if you consider regular milk chocolate, Chocolate, or if you are not occasionally partial to white chocolate (as I am) and very dark chocolate (which I

---

3 Posted Friday 17 May, 2013 at 1200 Hrs.

also like). Most people likely imagine milk chocolate, with its creamy, medium brown hue, whenever they say "chocolate," or at least my neighbors do.

What I am certain of is that Chocolate is not a beagle, because he's a hybrid, something between a pointer and a mutt. Mixed race, if you will, like me. When he first arrived next door, a pup from the pound, he was uncontrollable but adorable. Now he is larger, less adorable, and somewhat tamed, although his memory for my scent is sporadic at best. Not unlike Mum's power of recall. Some days, it's clear she has no idea who I am and probably does not believe either of her/my employees when they say I am her daughter. But I do not dislike having Chocolate as a neighbor; I just dislike the condition of our habitation, which is different from that percentage[4] of respondents among my fellow citizens who abhor persons of other races.

I think perhaps Hongkongers have forgotten what it's like to live in doghouses. They knew how to once, as squatters on hillsides in rickety shacks that were either washed away by typhoons or razed by the uncontrollable progress of fires. Some Hongkongers still live in doghouses: cages that rent for an extraordinarily high cost if reckoned on the price per square foot. There are also rooftop tenements—that is, the only name for these "rental properties"—illegal boxes to house Pakistani or Nepali service workers in Tsim Sha Tsui.

4 In subsequent news report, the exact percentage is a subject of dispute although Hong Kong still remains high on the scale around this issue, regardless, when compared to elsewhere. Statistical accuracy is, after all, a fluid notion.

Oh yes, said the realtor, *you can get good rental income from these six current tenants to cover the mortgage.* Yes, I thought, to pay for the overpriced flat below, owned by a Hong Kong Cantonese—that majority racial group—at a "good" address in a "civilized" neighborhood, while people live illegally in squalor above you.

At least Chocolate and I have a spacious rooftop, even if we do not always wish to be there.

In summer, I was dark chocolate as a child. Pigmentation. Indonesian blood mixed with Chinese. A fondness for sea and sun. Skin that did not easily burn. Being dark was natural for me except when regarded by most Hong Kong Chinese, and I learned to moderate my hue if I did not want to be the target of devilish cruelty. Perhaps that is why the survey was no surprise to me. Yet even an advocate for minority rights in Hong Kong was quoted as saying she was surprised by the survey's result. Ah, sweet naiveté! I too would prefer to believe in the fundamental humanity of my neighbors in my birth city, the city I keep trying to exit, *stage left,* like some discontented wildcat.

Do we dislike a place because it's too familiar, not familiar enough, or simply because someplace else compels us with its siren lure?

There used to be a bar in Tsim Sha Tsui called Someplace Else. The few times I went there, trying to find a hang in this city, it felt uncomfortable, isolating, unlike the bars of New York. Given its location by the harbor, it attracted an international crowd, which should have suited me. In time I learned that most bars in Hong Kong could never be like those in New York, and I gave up expecting that familiarity. This was when I was still "moving back," a physical and mental process that lasted around six or seven years, including the first two or so years *after* I'd already moved into the rooftop doghouse. Call me slow, but I wanted to hold onto the belief that bars were congenial places, where the bartender would become my intimate stranger-friend, the way they did in New York. Most of the bartenders in Tsim Sha Tsui are Filipino or Chinese, not American, so perhaps it is about nationality if not race, about a different kind of human (if not universal) experience here in this so-called "world city" that differs from that other world city, New York. Bartenders in New York may be any race, or nationality, given the city's multicultural character. This is something Hong Kong, with its 95% ethnic Chinese (mostly Cantonese) population, will never, ever be, not if it can help it.

Or perhaps it's because Hong Kong only recently raised its minimum wage from a pittance to a pittance-plus in this city of one the highest income disparities in the world.

We eat a lot of cake here, washed down by tea.

I share a doghouse in New York with my partner. That's what we named his railroad flat in Chelsea. It's narrow and small and if it had a roof would look like Snoopy's home. We are of different races; he is Caucasian—white chocolate—and likes dark, bitter chocolate that is not too sweet. Neither poses a problem, his race nor his chocolate preference. Our neighbors are many shades: white, brown, black. Disaster has yet to strike us on account of this.

A dark-skinned Sri Lankan acquaintance here in Hong Kong recently had his home's rental lease terminated after some twenty years. The owner sold the flat. He is a professional who paid his rent on time and had what he describes as a cordial relationship with his Cantonese landlady. Yet she gave him less than a month's notice. It was not an illegal act, just questionable, if we gave a dog's poop about human decency.

Whenever he showed up, in person, to try to rent a new flat, it was astonishing how rapidly the flat was "no longer available."

Are minority rights an oxymoron? Or just another fluid notion?

The frighteningly increased and ever increasing density of urban life in the 21st century is merely another insoluble problem of life on this planet. There are myriad others. Unanticipated meteors. Uncontrollable weather patterns. Lack of access to clean water. Inexplicable terrorist attacks wherever crowds gather for peaceful, recreational, or even ordinary daily activities, like commuting to work or conducting a war.

This city's density is no longer news. What it does mean, however, is that we are highly susceptible to pandemics. SARS, for example, or avian flu.

Or racism.

It's a kind of mind disease[5], I think, and is perhaps not the citizenry's fault since who knows from what or whom they might have contracted such illness. Floating dead swine in nearby rivers[6]. Cognitively impaired citizens masquerading as intelligentsia—one senior local government official recently proclaimed, *the way to avoid rape is for women not to get drunk.*[7] Surely, this had to be a symptom of mental impairment, and who knows how many more citizens of that ilk might be freely roaming our streets, infecting others?

After all, there are those who say the mind disease of democracy has also invaded our streets, infecting our youth, stirring up passions that should remain hidden. Some local academic will do a research study soon, undoubtedly, to confirm the veracity of this latest phenomenon.

---

5 Apparently, The Daily Show, presently hosted by John Oliver in Jon Stewart's absence, agrees with me on racism as a form of disease, which perhaps suggests that a true "universal" for humankind is how easily we succumb to contagion.
6 We refrain from showing photos of this phenomenon in Shanghai in order not to upset your digestive system as you dine on swine in the 5-star restaurant nearby, washed down by wine.
7 Fact. Look it up. Sadly, I kid you not.

Editors' Note: The following began on a new page and we chose to read it as a separate piece, although it echoes some of what appeared in the earlier pages. It was difficult to ascertain the writer's editorial intent because, despite the neat handwriting, there was no indication that the writer intended this for publication. On the cover of the notebook, this sentence was inscribed in capitals: **NO PERSON SHALL ALIGHT OR ATTEMPT TO ALIGHT OR ENTER OR ATTEMPT TO ENTER THIS NOTEBOOK EXCEPT BY WAY OF THE PROPER GANGPLANK.**[8] *We have been unable to decipher its meaning and wish we could ask the writer.*

---

8 It is possible that this language was paraphrased from signage on the vessels of the Star Ferry, circa 1960s to '70s, since replaced by marginally more comprehensible English, or something approximating English.

Anon.
Doghouse Rhapsody

At this very moment, there is a secret medical research study which has been submitted to the government for review, one that names uncontrollable racism an infectious disease in Hong Kong. It proposes a scientific name for the condition in order not to arouse undue emotional response and protest by the public should the facts ever be made known. **HK1-365-6**: The first specifically Hong Kong *disease of the mind* that can be in a person's system 365 days a year (with 6 for the intercalated leap), and is described as *a benign condition that flares up inexplicably, usually only for brief periods, not unlike a terrorist attack. Melting ice on the forehead of the afflicted individual can afford some relief.*

This research was paid for by a private sponsor, a global soft-drink brand, as a corporate social responsibility (CSR) measure, since CSR is all the rage and well funded.

To attempt to contain, if not cure, this disease, there is a proposal attached as an addendum to the medical research study. It seems promising. The document is currently making the rounds of government—which, as we know, will take a considerable length of time, given the filibustering tendency of our lawmakers. It is also likely to get buried, or vastly reconfigured if ever approved and released, which is why I have chosen to make it public now. In addition to fatigue at the city's racism epidemic, I am also fed up of one too many high-level deals conducted behind the closed doors of our government's offices.

This entire document came into my possession, although I am not at liberty to disclose how, except to say that it is from a whistle-blower of the highest moral character, someone well positioned to know all the facts. I have interviewed him intensively and have no reason to doubt the veracity of the document. As a permanent resident of this city, I have every reason to want only the best for Hong Kong, which is why I have chosen to share the modest, one-page proposal—because this could be a way to transform our city into a truly world-class one and a better place to live. It also will not overly tax the mental capacity of a populace unused to reading and who must digest, on a daily basis, entirely too much news that is, for the most part, incomprehensible.

*

PROPOSED LEGISLATION
(code name: "Doghouse Rhapsody")

Proposal: The Government of Hong Kong must pass legislation to transfer citizens who exhibit symptoms of the racism disease (hereinafter HK1-365-6) into a giant public space known as "The Doghouse," and keep them there for a minimum of three to a maximum of thirty days (excluding Sundays and "red day" public holidays). During that time, they will be fed and treated humanely, like domesticated dogs, but will be muzzled so that they may not speak, although fluids may continue to be ingested with a straw. Each person will be placed alone inside a metal structure, similar to a kennel or cage dwelling, but one that is equipped with a private portable toilet to maintain some semblance of human dignity. After all, we Hongkongese are no longer "running dogs" of the British, just floating swine of the Chinese.

Rationale: Hong Kong has a relatively law-abiding citizenry. Since many cannot suppress their auto-prejudicial disorders once they are infected with HK1-365-6, such a law, if passed, will be easy to enact. If those infected persons had a moment of silence in exile, they might reflect and learn to control their xenophobic seizures.

Implementation: Those who exhibit symptoms of HK1-365-6 will be herded into a giant doghouse in a public venue. The song "I'd Like to Teach the World to Sing (In Perfect Harmony" will be broadcast 24/7 in Cantonese, Putonghua, and English, our three official languages, in order to persuade them to sign a statement promising never to be cruel to anyone of a different race ever again. Only then will the they no longer be forced to listen to the musical broadcast. Length of stay will be commensurate with a willingness to sign said statement at any time after the first three days of quarantine.

*

This proposal is modest in its concision. I instantly recognized its elegant logic. A doghouse is *such* an obvious solution. Hongkongers love and adore their dogs—perhaps, at times, more than their children (who, according to another recent survey, are the most spoilt and over-indulged in the world and are therefore insufferable brats). Although there was no such question in the other survey, I suspect that if asked, Hongkongers probably would prefer dogs as neighbors over persons of a different race. If the number of dogs of all breeds resident in my largely mono-racial neighborhood is any indicator, then this notion may be valid.

This may also have something to do with the corporate sponsor wishing to acquire the rights to use Snoopy for their advertising, as a current Twitter rumor suggests. The only hint of this is that the document does say the design of the doghouse should be at the discretion of the sponsor. This is not the most egregious example of capitalistic imperialism. A giant doghouse in, say, the Hong Kong Coliseum, with a large inflatable Snoopy on its roof, might be viewed as an art installation, and thus a desirable contribution to local culture. This is a far, far, better thing than construction of yet another luxury residential complex, approved by our government to profit its favorite developer tycoon, as most of these sit empty for a long, long time, the repositories of money laundered for their absentee owners on the other side of that bamboo border. The doghouse will be full, easily, within a month after completion.

Besides, doesn't everyone here love Snoopy, since he passes that critical test of an adorable lack of meaning? In Hong Kong, China, the evolution from solidity to liquidity of creative images, brands, trademarks, *et al* happens with remarkable ease.

There is literary precedent. In Saramago's *Blindness*, those afflicted with the sudden onset of blindness were rounded up and confined by the municipal government in a large building. This quarantine was to contain possible infection. One day, they were all miraculously cured and could be released back into the city.

The same could happen to those afflicted by racism in Hong Kong.

In any case, the proposal is workable, I believe, and would be relatively painless to implement, as Hongkongers also favor large, peaceful, lawful assemblies for protest, except when the police (or security on university campuses) get over-excited and use undue force. After all, Occupy Hong Kong, while painful for some, will, if the government has its way (as it increasingly does) enter into our history redacted and revised, painlessly flushed away from memory. Transferring diseased individuals into a gigantic doghouse need not require undue force if no police or security are involved, thus preventing public protest. Hong Kong's domesticated dogs (which are the majority species these days, as opposed to the rabid strays of yesteryear that used to be the majority) could be trained as sheepdogs, and released to gently herd these mentally damaged individuals into their temporary dwelling. Given the number of Australians who seem to want to work in this city, it should not be hard to find those with experience in training sheepdogs willing to apply for the lucrative, government-salaried positions to do so. After all, the British have long raided local coffers for government jobs of considerably less value to our city, so it's time to give the rest of the Commonwealth a fair shake as well. Besides Australians, New Zealanders might also choose to apply. This would offer work opportunities for international professionals here and further enhance Hong Kong's image as a world city, which would please the Tourist Association and other official mythmakers.

In fact, the more I think about this, the more I like it. The document is so careful in its avoidance of blame. By naming this condition a disease, people can immediately see that no one is saying it's their *fault* for being racist. As with any communicable disease, a racist might simply have caught a virus from some random carrier. This city has millions of tourists passing through each year—the majority from the Chinese mainland—so chances are good this would happen, the way cholera has returned after a long absence. After all, the medical research report only states that this disease has been found to be *infectious in Hong Kong*. It does not say how or where the disease originated (a particularly sensitive approach to scientific research reporting, I felt). Infection might be due to any number of environmental factors, including, but not limited to: general air and noise pollution (blameworthy for most ills here); migratory patterns of butterflies (of which this city has numerous species so these could be carriers); an inflatable giant yellow rubber ducky that mysteriously deflated in the Hong Kong harbor (viruses adhere to rubber); Chinese cigarette butts in our garbage, waterways, and landfills (who knows what fake substances these might contain, with what unknown properties, since lamb sold in some parts of China is really rat meat).

I lose count.

The devil, as everyone knows, wears Prada, and we have more than our share of that and myriad other designer brands along our shores and in rapid transit across our borders, having not suffered the alarming fate of the tinned milk powder black market that was vanquished by local authorities, along with the students who once slept on our streets for months in the name of democracy. An Umbrella Movement. History is fluid. Life is the here and now. Words are just words so we might as well lose count.

From the streets of Occupied Hong Kong, Mong Kok, November, 2014

Lyrics to "Freedom Flower" by a tent on the streets of Occupied Hong Kong, Mong Kok, November 2014

COINCIDENCE

for Marie

ONCE, when she was almost seven, she overheard
Number Six Auntie say to Grandma Chan, but
she has her eyes and you wait and see, her body as
well. Once she starts menstruating it'll be all over. You can't
change blood. They were all getting ready for mass, an oblig-
atory one, the Immaculate Conception, although about the
exactness of this moment, her memory slip-slides. What she
does remember with absolute certainty is that during the con-
secration, a sudden flash of knowing—Six Auntie was talking
about her, she had to be. She immediately asked Pa if they
could go home because she wasn't feeling well, which was only
a partial untruth because her brain was vomiting. Afterward,
she stuck to the lie of a physical ailment. Pa let it go, even
though she suspected he knew it was a lie, and he never even
insisted on making her go to the doctor's.

It's not my blood, not my blood her colleague exclaims as
they stare together at a still-damp stain on the white cloth
covering the coffee tray in the conference room. Anna Mag-

nolia removes the cloth and shoves it quickly into a drawer before the executives arrive. Her colleague Snow is pale, and checks her hands and arms again and again, making sure there isn't a wound. *Don't worry about it,* Anna Magnolia says, *probably one of the cleaners,* but even as she says this, she knows that's not true.

The managing director arrives first along with Anna Magnolia's boss Alexander and they smile at both women. The MD is always early: *leading by example,* Alexander likes to tell staff and few are ever late for meetings at this investor relations firm. Soon the meeting is underway, and she takes her place at the conference table to make sure the recorder works properly. It doesn't but this isn't evident till later. Snow takes notes for minutes which she'll later compile with difficulty, begging for help because parts of the recording will be garbled. Anna Magnolia transcribes the proceedings word-for-word in shorthand. Her boss Alexander expressed surprise at this skill when he hired her four years prior, saying, *it's unusual these days since everyone uses PCs, no one dictates anymore,* and she had replied, *I just found it interesting and decided to learn it well.* At this job, her shorthand has proven an asset, because an accurate record of what everyone says, both for themselves and their clients, is paramount. And she's fast, exceptionally so.

That night, though, as she tosses around in bed, Snow's exclamation dogs her. *Not my blood, not my blood.* It wasn't blood as was obvious when she brought the cloth to the pantry to wash it. Snow is young, only twenty-two and constantly in a flap, tremulous when confronted with the tiniest problem.

Today's hadn't even been a problem; a non-problem, more like. The only reason she has a position at all, Anna Magnolia thinks, is because her father is who he is. Plus, she's pretty. The younger guys are always eyeing her. She'll last a year at most, and then she'll marry someone from her set, retire to society tai-taihood, and no longer waste the firm's resources and time..

An uncomfortable heat warms her body and she throws off the covers. And then she shivers. This hot-cold-hot rush happens frequently of late. Why should this morning upset her so much? After all, Snow's just another executive trainee, and the pattern is the same for all of them. These trainees whom Alexander complains about to her, saying *oh god, not another girl,* and rolls his eyes, as he did this afternoon when he came to her office. He was staring at her when he said that, hard, too hard, and Anna Magnolia felt that other heat, the one between her legs which she always tries desperately to stop but can't. Meanwhile Alexander was saying, *thank goodness you're a grownup, Anna, a real woman.* She can't help it, blushes every time he says that as he leaned in a little too close, staring at her breasts, *Don't be ashamed of the truth,* he reassured. *You're far more competent, and intelligent, than all those princess-dolls.* And then he takes that deep breath he does as he continued gazing at her, a gaze so nakedly painful that she can barely stand it as she waited for him to say something, anything. Every time, until it's become almost a pattern, he'll abruptly turn around without another word and walk away as he did again today.

It is well past five before she dozes off for maybe forty

minutes of dream-wracked sleep before the alarm rings.

In the morning, Pa is chatty. She has asked their helper to prepare his favorite breakfast, a slice of ham and omelet on toast. He drinks his milky tea, asks how much of a raise she expects because her annual review is very good, excellent in fact. *Alexander Kwan thinks highly of you. I'm very proud you're doing so well,* he says. She nods, looks down at her plate, wracked by a plethora of emotions she cannot name. Pa's mention of her boss ravages her insides into a kind of rigor mortis; her earlier nightmare—Alexander back when Michael—that unaccountable heat flush races through her, one she forces herself to control. *You must thank him,* Pa is saying. *I'll try to remember to make conversation this Sunday after Mass.* She barely registers what he says, murmurs something about Alexander being the most thoughtful boss, to which Pa replies, *yes, we don't forget what he did for you. A compassionate boss when you had those problems, never complaining when you needed time off.* Head bowed, she finishes breakfast. The problem of Michael is never completely over, even when it is.

The MTR suffers a delay and she is trapped mid-commute, waiting for the train to start moving again. Hers is the next stop. Annoying. Such delays are usually quickly resolved, although as she checks her phone for emails and texts from work, Anna Magnolia thinks that there seem to be a lot more delays lately. There is the daily meeting notice from Alexander's executive assistant Jun-li. She likes this younger colleague who fills her in on all the latest office gossip. Jun-li has only been with Alexander half a year, having moved from Beijing with her husband when he transferred to the Hong

Kong office of one of their firm's clients. She is funny and sociable, interested in more than the trivial nonsense over which too many of her colleagues waste saliva. And she knows her own mind, even has her own stylish dress sense, and doesn't simply fall in line with the black, black and more black boring uniform of the local girls and boys at work. Anna Magnolia is looking forward to their lunch date today.

Five more minutes and the train still isn't moving. This delay is beginning to upset her. She is a patient woman, and these exigencies of urban life normally don't bother her, but on this day, breakfast is not sitting well and Pa looked a little worried this morning (although when she asked what the problem was, he replied, as he always does, *there's nothing wrong, don't you worry yourself unnecessarily*). Pa is considerate, like her, unlike her mother who died inconveniently not long after giving birth to Anna Magnolia, but who lived long enough to curse her with this name from the American South. A name out of sync with who she is. The train lurches forward. Anna Magnolia loses her balance and bangs into a girl who glares at her. She is about to apologize, but the girl looks away, says loudly to her friend, *devil woman SO clumsy* and they both laugh. Anna Magnolia tells herself, ignore them, forget it, but this morning, she simply cannot stop herself and exclaims, 你唔好亂叫我做鬼婆! *don't you dare careless-call me devil woman!* Her explosive scold is loud, and the two girls, startled by her fluent, native-speaker Cantonese and, publicly shamed, hurry away embarrassed to another part of the carriage. The train doors open at her stop and Anna Magnolia dashes out, and now, it's more than breakfast or Pa's worry sitting badly as she heads towards the office tower, ascends its lift and rushes into her office which has "Anna Chan - Client Services Manager" etched on the glass door. Two bullpen colleagues exchange glances as her door almost slams shut, breaking the morning's silence.

Work is work, and shortly before noon, she has had enough of Snow's whining. She texts Jun-li: *time? where?* The reply: *sorry sorry sorry something came up* 😟 *tomorrow ok ?* She texts back: *ok*. She is more than disappointed though, and feels herself becoming really, really upset. This is ridiculous, she tells herself; trying to calm down, she decides on an early lunch—a perk of working for Alexander, who is lenient about schedules—and, grabbing her purse, heads to the lift bank via a quick stop at the toilet. As she emerges from the stall, she sees the departing figure of Jun-li. She washes her hands quickly, hoping to catch her. When she emerges, Jun-li is nowhere in sight, so she goes towards the lift bank but stops, shocked at the sight of Jun-li and Alexander entering an empty lift together, their bodies close, his hand against her lower back, touching her the way that he has never, ever touched Anna Magnolia.

The first time Anna Magnolia Chan had more than merely an inkling that she was not all Chinese was the day she started Primary One. It was a local Catholic girls' school, the elite one all her cousins attended as well as her aunts, way back when. At recess, three girls came up to her, giggling, asking, *nei hai mutt yeh ah?* She blinked at them, silently uncomprehending. What did they mean by that, calling her a *yeh?* She wasn't a thing. One of the girls yanked her ponytail, twirled the dark brown strand in her finger, and exclaimed, *gaam luen!* And then they ran away, laughing. She asked Pa that evening, *why is my hair so curly?* Pa said, *what do you mean?* She said none of her girl cousins, who were all older, had such curly hair, and then she named Pa's sisters one by one: Three and Six Aunties, who also had long hair that wasn't curly; only Two, Four, and Five Aunties had curls, but their hair was short and permed. *And,* she added excitedly, *Number One Auntie who cuts her hair real short like a boy's has super straight hair, it sticks up like a toilet brush.* It was something Pa said about One Auntie that always made her laugh, and then she added, *like you, Pa.* She had been leaning forward as she spoke, and now she sat back, awaiting an explanation. Pa was silent but then beamed a big smile, *that's because yours is lucky hair, it curls on its own.* Which partly satisfied her. She was six and a half. But by the middle of that year she had been called *jaap jung* more than once and cried herself to sleep over the taunts (*your blood's mixed, you're not real Chinese*), afraid to say anything to Pa or her cousins or aunts so as not to annoy them. Bad enough being the baby of the family, but she was *not* a crybaby. It was not till after the Immaculate Conception mass that she was finally told about her mother.

She is right now in shock, comparable to the way she felt as a child when told her mother was Caucasian, an American from New Orleans, Louisiana. A stunningly beautiful, good Catholic woman, the daughter of missionaries in China, and sexy, whom Pa fell in love with and married against his family's wishes—meaning without Grandma's approval. Anna

Magnolia assumes Jun-li to be happily married because she's never said anything bad about her husband. So why are she and Alexander skulking, leaving too early for lunch, looking like they're committing adultery? Anna Magnolia's insides churn, whipped into a froth of violent moral recriminations. Alexander is Catholic, even if Jun-li is not, and he really, really ought to know better.

"Are you okay?" Snow gazes at her, concerned. "Are you feeling ill?"

She sees the scratches on her forearms where she's been clawing herself and quickly clutches her arms tightly, says "I'm fine," strides towards the lift, and bangs on the call button, hurting her hand. Snow glances at the two other trainees in her entourage who, eyes rolling, tap at their temples as they all walk away.

The spring day is warm as Anna Magnolia exits to the outdoor concourse, her early lunch plan derailed. There is a little wind and the whitecaps are visible out on the harbor. She rubs her forearms, digs around in her bag for hand lotion to rub on her skin. What is wrong with this day? Why is everything topsy-turvy? She wants to call Pa, to demand that he tell her the truth, that he is probably in debt, having bet too heavily at the races and lost. He will have to beg Grandma to bail him out again and endure her nagging. It shouldn't be such a big deal, given how wealthy the family is, but when it comes to money, Grandma Chan is a tightwad. Grandpa, long deceased, amassed a fortune in properties. A fucking *gigantic* fortune. All the Chans live off rental income, which is fine for Pa's sisters who can do good works and raise their children well (as Grandma says); but a man, now a man's different because he must have a profession. *I do have one,* Pa tells her. *I'm a professional gambler and lover of beautiful women.* Which he is. He's never remarried, attracts and discards the women on the social register like some kind of serial murderer, and, once she understood more fully about her mother, Anna Magnolia consoled herself that at least her parents truly had been in love.

And wasn't it love the night she and Alexander worked late last week when he said—*Anna Chan, you'll make someone a good wife one day*—hadn't he meant to tell her, discreetly, that he was falling in love with her the way she already had with him? She was seated at her desk, her back to him when he spoke; and she spun her chair around, gazing up at him; and the look in his eyes was tender, without that tumultuous edge he too often trained on her. It was so unexpected, so startling, to have him say out loud what she craved so badly to hear, this desire for much more than merely a boss's approval. Alexander, early 30s, single, not gay, a UST MBA, and from a respectable Cantonese family—the father a successful jeweler and his mother on the boards of several charities that raised funds for natural-disaster victims in China—with enough wealth to satisfy Grandma. And devoutly Catholic. The perfect candidate for a husband to a Chan girl.

The chiming of bells, a person-specific ringtone. Six Auntie.

Wei, you need to talk to your father. Grandma is livid. Six Auntie, the youngest sister is a year older than Pa, the only boy among the Chans. Their proximity in the family hierarchy means that Six Auntie is almost like a mother to her, this woman who, shamefully, has been unable to bear children, and remains forever the target of Grandma's passive wrath. Six Auntie told her about her mother and comforted her when Anna Magnolia cried, horrified that she was half *gwai* after all, a *jaap jung*, something she had suspected since she was four but refused to believe. The Chan family is Cantonese, and *very* traditionally Chinese, which is how Anna Magnolia was raised. She can recite the Confucian Analects but is also fluent in English of course, and is cosmopolitan and worldly, having traveled abroad the way everyone who grew up well in British Hong Kong does. Things haven't changed a whole lot in Chinese Hong Kong, except that these days, she speaks Mandarin more often, although when she does, she wonders if this *Putonghua* will ever really be her tongue. But all her pride and sense of being, her very existence is wrapped up in being someone whose real world is right here, in this city, in this way of living, as part of an educated, cultured, comfortably upper middle-class Cantonese family who must marry and procreate only with their own. When she shrieked *no* yan *will ever want me!* repeating what she had heard the adults say about mixed-race children, Six Auntie consoled, *shh, shh, don't worry, things are different now, Hong Kong* yan *aren't so close-minded anymore.* But even as she stopped sniffling, she knew, in that instance, her future would not be like her aunts and their husbands or most of her cousins. She is and always will be an outsider, able to retain the privilege of being a Chan but never truly one of them. Like Pa.

"I'll talk to him," she promises Six Auntie, who is already

veering off to another subject, the cousin's wedding banquet next week. It is the marriage of Three Auntie's son, the smart one, a Cheung whose father is an oncologist at the Prince of Wales Hospital out in Sha Tin, about which Grandma grumbles, *so far away, why doesn't he have his practice on the Hong Kong side, closer to where we all live,* although she does more or less approve of the bride-to-be, who is American-ABC but does speak Cantonese well enough and is respectful. Six Auntie says Cheung is a good father and reminds her that Three Auntie just flipped a couple more contracts on flats, amassing an even larger fortune from her share of the family's money, which only partially mollifies Grandma. Anna Magnolia is distracted by all this family chatter which circles around the upcoming wedding and Grandma because everything, if you're a Chan, everything always comes back to Grandma. Six Auntie is, despite everything, Grandma's favorite and she's protected Anna Magnolia, carving out a space for her in the rigidly conservative clan, teaching her how to secure her perch, despite who she is and how she looks.

So you will wear that dress, right? It's perfect for your figure and coloring, Six Auntie is saying. *The others would kill to be able to wear it as well as you will.* The outfit appeared a month ago, an expensive gift from Six Auntie. A strapless plunging top that mermaids its way to a softly draped, calf-length skirt, slit to the knee. Pearl grey with an inside-out pink lining and matching shawl. It will show off far more cleavage than Anna Magnolia has ever bared. Unlike all her female cousins and girlfriends, Anna Magnolia has never, ever owned a padded bra or considered breast implants. She is completely, naturally a 35C. Later, much later, when she is happily in love at last, a flash of realization will dawn: she has never desired or needed eyelid surgery either. But that is much later in her life, and right now, she is unhappily in love, as she has been for almost two years, with Alexander Kwan.

And add the diamond-pearl necklace we got last year with the earrings. You'll look stunning.

"I rather doubt that," she says and changes tracks to the flower arrangement for church that Sunday, something to distract Six Auntie. By the time the call is over, Anna Magnolia is no longer thinking about lunch.

Surviving the Chan Domain, which is how Pa refers to their mission in the family, rules Anna Magnolia's life. *We're their sore spot,* Pa says, *the zit they can't erase no matter how hard they try.* When she turned thirteen and began menstruating (*why so late,* Two Auntie says, *all girls get the month's crossing very early now, as young as eight or nine),* even Four Auntie paid attention. Four Auntie who usually ignores family gossip piped up with *oh ho, Baby Brother will have to be a father for real now!* She didn't understand the fuss at first, or all the knowing glances from her older girl cousins. Pa finally sat her down and said, *you're a very sexy girl.* Too *sexy.*

He told her Sunday morning after the Cancer Society ball. She had been so excited about being allowed to go, the kind of fancy social event her older girl cousins talked about. This was smack in the midst of the mad nineties, when Hong Kong was still British: the economy was thriving; the money flowed and was flaunted. Her father and aunts sat on the boards of numerous charities and societies, and December meant balls every weekend, despite Advent. Six Auntie took her to have her first evening gown made. It was a Diana dress, a copy of the Catherine Walker ivory silk crepe Her Royal Highness had worn earlier that year at the Malaysian state banquet, although hers was pink, not ivory. *Classic,* Pa said approvingly as he gave her his arm to escort her to their table. She felt so grown up, her hair pinned up by Three Auntie, who was good at such things—cajoled into helping by Six Auntie, of course—and her makeup perfectly applied. The lovely pale pink material wrapped her shoulders and gathered at her breasts, allowing a discreet décolletage. She was asked to dance by some of the sons of Pa's friends, and one older Englishman as well. At first she hesitated but Pa said, *it's okay, Geoffrey's harmless even if he's still single.* It was her princess moment. Her cousins treated her nicely, complimenting her, saying she looked pretty, instead of calling her *sai muih*, a dismissal of the youngest among them as they usually did.

Right now, in her funk haze, she barely realizes she's being addressed by the English voice saying, "Anna Chan, isn't it? Wai-man's daughter?"

His face is familiar, this Englishman standing in front of her. He's forty-ish, possibly older, grey edging his temples, but is tanned and remarkably fit. "It is, isn't it? I thought I recognized you. Geoffrey Carder, from your father's solicitors?"

The familiar stranger snaps her back to herself and she locates her tongue and manners. Smiles. "Oh, of course, what a coincidence."

"Yes, isn't it?" His smile is generous. "Lovely day to be

outside."

He asks after Pa, then remarks that it's been *oh at least two years, more,* since she and he had last seen each other, and recalls, *that medical charity thing, spina bifida wasn't it? We had a dance.* She does recalls that ball and says yes, indeed they did meet over a dance. There is a brief silence and he adds, *the event with that extravagantly expensive but tasteless décor. They couldn't have raised much money in the end.* They both laugh at the memory. Anna Magnolia sees him then, in a tux standing next to his wife—what was her name?—whose bright orange and lime colored gown had been odd, uncharacteristically loud, and what she also recalls is that when she glanced back at their table behind hers at the end of the night, Geoffrey looked out of sorts, fatigued perhaps, but more like upset, but that his wife—Charmaine? Charlotte?—was laughing, raising a flute, and spilling champagne, and that the rest of the party at his all-Caucasian table were in very high spirits.

"And is," the name hovers, lands on her tongue, "Charlaine well?" There were no children.

"We're… divorcing." In the brief pause, she saw in his expression the same one of that night, two and a half years earlier—in 2013, she is positive, a charity extravaganza where the entire ballroom had been decorated with stage sets for over-the-top tableaux performed by women on the committee, all draped in Greco-Roman slink, eyes wide shut, an excuse to bare backs and legs and as much of their breasts as they dared.

"Oh. I'm sorry."

"Don't be. It's the best thing and should have happened a long time ago." Now he flashes a brighter smile, eyes aglow.

"And you? How's," he stops. "I'm sorry, I've forgotten your fiancé's name. Although I imagine he's your husband now?"

Her face flushes—what she despises about her pale complexion—even though she strives to contain it, and she can tell it's obvious to him. "Michael. He isn't. Either my fiancé or husband." It's the first time she's said this to anyone outside the family, having avoided seeing even her best girlfriends as much as possible after the engagement was called off. In the Chan clan, everyone saw, naturally, when Michael's face was splashed across the Chinese gossip press cavorting at Propaganda, in the arms of—and here she refuses to even *think* his name—the gay Mando-pop singer from Beijing. Which is where Michael Wong is now, shacked up with his lover.

But Geoffrey—this *sai yan-gwailo*, this foreigner-local, as she herself is—he couldn't have known, though she can see from his *oh-fuck* face that her shameful history has suddenly dawned upon him, because the story had sped across their social grapevine and everyone knew. Everyone. She, on the other hand, *should* have known, the way any full-blooded Chinese would have known why Michael Wong, from a well-to-do local family, who belonged to the Jockey Club *and* the American Club, and was good looking to boot, chose to be with her, the one who did not belong. Despite their place in this world she and Michael both inhabited, seemingly with such ease, it was only for as long as each could totter, precariously, before the inevitable implosion.

She and Geoffrey look at each other properly for the first time. The sensation for Anna Magnolia is akin to the first time she properly studied a photograph of her mother and told herself, *so there you are, you and me.* She had been nine.

"Well," he says. "I guess we've both… bled?"

Anna Magnolia's day is now just topsy but a little less turvy. It is settling into a new, unfamiliar calm. The flush drains from her face. "You could say that. The bleeding does stop, I suppose. Eventually."

"So what are you doing the rest of this afternoon?"

And she recalls how, when she was thirteen and a half at her first society ball with Pa, Geoffrey had invited her to dance and she found him kind of sexy, although she never dared say that aloud to anyone in the family, not about a *gwailo.* Especially an older man. All the Chan girls know better than to be seduced by The Other. She didn't quite know what it meant then, this new idea of a sexy male, just as her father's explanation the next morning, that *she* was sexy, *too* sexy, did not make sense to her for a long time. Until Alexander Kwan. She knew the way he looked at her was… which is why she had thought that with Alexander, it would be okay to give in, fine to let go and just drown. Except he never made a move, despite the many opportunities she engineered towards that end. Never. Unlike Alexander, Michael, the one who had made the move, Michael had simply been beautiful.

Geoffrey's eyes are still disarming, even now, but his gaze is polite, unlike Alexander's. Breeding is what she's always liked about him, never calling attention to himself, simply exuding his essence without guile. The way she knows she does, the way she can't help being, unlike Pa and most of the Chan clan who structure exuberance and other inconvenient emotions into acceptable compartments.

She says, "I have to go back to the office. Although," and she glances up at the heavens, "it *is* a beautiful day, isn't it?"

"Yes," he agrees. "Would be a shame to ignore it, don't you think?"

That afternoon, she calls in sick and Alexander sounds annoyed, although what he says is *get some rest and get better soon.* Anna Magnolia doesn't—get better, that is—and takes the rest of the week off, knowing she'll be leaving her boss in the lurch at this exceptionally busy moment. Her cousin, Two Auntie's eldest daughter, will write her the medical excuse she'll need for HR. Which she'll submit whether or not she stays on at the firm. As she tells Pa Saturday morning over breakfast, she is considering a change of scene, and would it be all right if she took a break—*goodness knows I have all this unused leave*—and went on holiday for a while, maybe to London, where she could look in on her cousin Ronson the artist—*the Artist of Plenty and Penury*, Pa dubs him—Four Auntie's youngest? The cousin who will never ever come home because he imploded and then exploded spectacularly well a really long time ago and no longer gives a shit about Grandma. *Of course*, Pa replies. *You should do whatever you feel like doing. I do.* She nods, looks up from her plate, and says, *by the way, guess who I ran into the other day?* And Pa is pleased to hear that Geoffrey is doing all right, finally resolving the messy divorce with *that woman*, and then he has a brainwave. Why doesn't Anna Magnolia invite Geoffrey to make up their table at the wedding next week, since it is one short because Mrs. Wang's husband was struck with shingles and has to be excused but this means the Wangs' *lai see* will pay for that seat.

When she says, *are you sure that's okay? Won't Uncle or Grandma complain,* Pa responds, *oh it's no problem, Grandma loves weddings and is always a dizzy-lizzie at the dinners, and will be all smiles at this one because the Cheung boy and your future cousin-in-law will perform the tea thing properly for all their American* gwailo *guests. Oh and I hear the bride has this grotesquely traditional* qipao, *one that is modeled on the one your Grandma herself wore when* she *was a blushing bride but do you imagine* her *blushing? Hah? Hah?* And Pa cackles, the way he does whenever the subject turns to Grandma. It is their private joke, one that always makes Anna Magnolia feel safe. *Besides, Three Auntie will be all sweet and considerate, fawning all over Grandma, and anyway, everyone likes Geoffrey. Everyone. He's harmless. Really, it's no problem.*

the city's stories we choose to tell

MARINER

AS soon as I was settled at the corner of the bar in the last empty seat, he flashed a warm, open smile. Friendly. I acknowledged him. It would have been rude not to even though the phone in my pocket was jumping, buzzing against my thigh. The trouble with soft fabric. "Excuse me," I said. *Of course she was running late, no need for apologies. Of course I'd wait.* I always wait for Mandi, who bought me these pants. And the boxers. It still surprises me that someone in fashion would be a free bird sort of girl.

I clicked off.

He asked, "Come here often?"

"Once in a while. Good location."

He gazed at the harbor and the island. Neon blinked against an unusually red sun.

"The view's spectacular." He continued gazing. "Heard about this bar forever and finally got here. It's been twelve years since I last landed in Hong Kong."

My wine arrived. He was drinking a large martini.

"So you live here?"

He wanted to talk. I wanted to read *The Economist.* The latest issue just pinged my inbox and I gazed at the screen with longing, briefly, before good manners interfered.

I faced him. "Yes. You a FedEx pilot?" That was a safe bet.

They were mostly FedEx pilots who frequented this happy hour to wolf down the generous servings of free steak sandwiches.

"UPS. Eighteen years and still standing."

"Didn't know the crew stayed here." The American five-star hotel chain that housed this bar has been here since my childhood. Back then, I never dreamed I'd be in it someday, and with money to burn. My parents sometimes stay here when they visit.

"We don't." He named some new hotel around the corner. Four stars, max. His complaints covered the next few conversational minutes. "It's taken me twelve years to land back here," he repeated.

He was wearing a blue and white checkered shirt and tan pants. Sandy-haired, fair-skinned, medium height, a little heavy but not yet obese, he had the kind of face that told you nothing. Amiable, pleasant enough, ordinary. Impossible to describe to the police after an incident. The boy next door who might be a serial killer. I did not want to ask about Vietnam. He looked about the right age for that nostalgia. The last one I asked got drunk and called me a gook. *That learned you,* Mandi had said, deliberately releasing her Southern drawl. I'm a mutt, seriously mixed, but often mistaken for Caucasian. Usually, the Americans passing through can't tell. I remained silent.

He didn't wait for my response. "I'm fifty-four, still flying and it took me all this time to get back here."

"When d'you fly out?"

"Tomorrow. Dubai and then after that Cologne and then

back home to Louisville. That's in Kentucky."

"I know that." Curt. Shouldn't have annoyed me but it did. I softened my tone. "My girlfriend's from Tennessee."

"You don't say? You sound English."

"Blame it on school."

He held out his hand. "Bobby."

"Dirk."

"You been to the U.S.?"

"A few times." In fact, I flew regularly to L.A. and Chicago, as well as down south, but I wasn't about to tell him the story of my life, or confess to my dual citizenship.

"We're in a terrible state." He finished off his drink and signaled another. "Terrible. I'm fifty-four and can't remember it ever being worse. I was born in '59."

Another bumpy ride. Where the hell was Mandi? She'd have shut him down in two seconds flat and he'd never know what happened. I swallowed another mouthful. Good Cab. French.

"There's no global warming," he continued. "It's just weather. I fly around the world, I should know. They're just talking garbage science to make money. Al Gore's a millionaire."

I nodded. It seemed the safer thing to do than reveal any political proclivities.

"And they're destroying the Constitution. When I was a boy, we knew our country's history, understood the second amendment for what it was. Now they just want to take away our guns and protection."

I nodded again. This one I wasn't even going to start.

Mandi's father hunts. I avoid becoming prey.

He was staring at my pants. Okay, I did think them overly gay-metro when she first made me put them on, but the fabric falls in place nicely. Mandi likes to grope and the soft material turns her on She makes *Sex in the City* seem like *Rebecca of Sunnybrook Farm*.

"And Obamacare will be the death of the country. There's no Social Security. But you and your girlfriend, you're still too young to worry about all that."

He was still staring at my pants. Wait, surely not? Since Mandi, my gaydar's ratcheted up a notch, but *this* one?

"Do you have kids?" I tried. Family was always a good picker-upper.

He brightened. "One boy. He's twenty-two."

I waited for the wallet album. Instead he said, "He's got to worry about his job. Manages a Radio Shack. Not like when I was a boy. I was born in '59. You could have dreams then."

I decided to skip the wife. Divorce, nasty, seemed too likely. "Did you always want to fly?"

He visibly brightened. "Yep. Ever since I was ten. Joined the Air Force when I was nineteen. That was the way to go. I should never have left, but you know, you retire. Seemed like the right thing to do at the time."

"You ever fly passenger?"

"Nope, always cargo. Don't like passenger. You don't want to fly people, they're too much trouble."

I glanced at my phone. Mandi was now ridiculously late. I excused myself for a toilet reprieve, even though I didn't really have to go. How had he guessed I was waiting for a girlfriend?

When I returned, he was gazing at the harbor. Waiting for the light show, I suspected. Everyone comes for the light show. Mandi wanted to when I told her I sometimes drank here. At 8pm, the buildings along the waterfront all come alive and emit this choreography of lights. I swear you can almost hear the dance track. It's a colossal waste of energy, but Mandi called me a party pooper for saying that. Maybe that's my real problem and why I drink more than I should.

The server waltzed by with a tray of mini steak sandwiches. Bobby took three. Clearly, he was doing dinner. He gestured toward me an avuncular *eat, eat*. What the hell, I might as well if she was going to be this late. We were clearly not going to make our seven thirty dinner reservation. I called the restaurant. Luckily, they know me there and it was a weekday so that got sorted. Plus it gave me a further reprieve from Bobby.

Bobby was starting on the second sandwich. "These are great," he said between bites. "I really wish I got here more often. It's been twelve years."

I was courting regret but asked anyway: "What did you do the last time you were here?"

He didn't answer right off, and I felt this strange surge of sadness. Perhaps his wasn't just compulsive chit-chat. Perhaps there really had been something, or someone, to remember. I thought about my parents, how they hated coming back after we moved to Essex when I was fourteen. How they complained about the pollution, the crowds, the price of everything, the problem of a rising China. How they finally shut up about my move back when they heard how much I could earn here *because* of China. Still earn, four years on.

"Walked by the harbor all evening, just taking in the sights. It was so beautiful. The sky was clear and it wasn't too hot. It was September. I flew to Brussels the next day."

He seemed calm, maybe even happy. I did the math: 9/11—that had to be it.

His moment of calm didn't last. "Nothing's been right since. Country's got no leadership. The last real leader we had was Reagan, y'know what I mean?" He paused. "But you're too young to remember him properly, aren't you?"

I'm actually older than I look, but there was no reason to enlighten him. I swallowed more wine.

"You're a college boy, aren't you?"

That was unexpected. "I went to university."

"You Chinese, you believe in education. It's a good thing."

Unnerved, I blinked. Mandi says I look more Chinese now than when we first met three years ago. It happens to our kind. Glancing down, I saw he wore a wedding band.

He barreled on. "My son, he didn't want to go to college, was never good at school. I told him to go, told him to try, but he wanted to get a job. Well he got a job at Radio Shack and worked his way up. Works hard, never misses a day of work. He's a good boy. His mother would have been proud. She was a great mom. But now, he may not have a job soon. How he'll pay his mortgage, I don't know. Everyone's becoming a part-timer in our dumb service economy. We don't *make* anything anymore. The whole country's gone to hell in a hand-basket."

His second martini was dangerously low.

"Me, I was born in '59. You could still have dreams then. Now I won't even have Social Security."

The light show began.

At the other end of the bar, Mandi was making her usual spectacular entrance. Male heads turned as she headed straight toward me. Tight, short skirt, a mass of ash-gold hair, lightly bronzed complexion, deep red lips, embers in her eyes, and long legs that did the runway stalk in her stilettos. Whether mouth, ass, or leg men, they all lust-gazed. An ego-gratifying girlfriend who loved me. The ring box was in my other pocket. What more should a boy want?

Bobby stared straight ahead at the lights, beaming over the harbor, lighting the evening sky.

She arrived, slid her oh-so-perfect body between his barstool and mine, and even before I could stand, had me in an embrace with *so sorry, so sorry, but you know how she is, such a yadda yadda loves the sound of her own voice.* Mandi is nothing if not effusive.

I gave her my seat, got her a Pinot Grigio, and for the next few minutes of chatter, Bobby did not need to exist in our universe.

By the time I looked at him again, he was paying his bill. He had moved his barstool over to make room for Mandi and me, regal in our corner. He stuck out his hand. "Bobby. You must be the girlfriend."

Mandi shook it. I couldn't help but admire those beautifully manicured nails. "Pleased to meet you, Bobby," she said in her best Southern drawl.

"Mandi. Nice to meet another Southerner out in these

parts." It was only then that it struck me he had a slight drawl too. Why hadn't I noticed? I usually pick up on these things.

"Dirk and Mandi," he began.

I cringed, waited. They always said it, these chaps of limited imagination. Their version of limey rhyme. *Dirk and Mandi, Mork and Mindy. Hahahaha.*

He stood up. "You kids. Lucky kids. You have a wonderful life."

I needed to say something. *Come back soon?* A detail from his diatribe dinged. The late wife. What to say? What should I say? But Mandi was chattering, her hands sliding touchy-feelingly around my sides, dangerously roving, muddling my concentration. She was the here and now, the start of the rest of my life. Bobby? Well, he'd find another victim.

Mandi twisted about in that way she does. It drives me wild. I turned to face the bar. She leaned against my arm, whispered, *maybe we could skip dinner?* Tempting. She is one hot girl, but tonight was my show. Yet my attention kept shifting to Bobby, there in my peripheral vision. I waited for his expression to change, wanting something more.

He turned and left. Didn't say goodbye. The ring box nudged my groin, reminding me of more urgent life.

Afterward, much later that night, after the most romantic dinner in the world, Mandi fell asleep, exhausted by love. I lay next to her awhile. After fifteen minutes, I got up and went to the living room of my perfect urban flat, rent paid by the bank that employed me. From up here, you can see the harbor. I squinted. Bobby was down there somewhere. Had to be. I needed him to be. Walking the harborfront where the light show had ended, against a sky that was no longer illuminated.

THE 15ᵀᴴ ANNUAL ANNIVERSARY

for Felix 弟弟 in eternity

HE had gone, against his better judgment, to their **high school class's 35ᵗʰ reunion dinner.** Only because F was persistent. His emails and Facebook bulletins during the past year had subtly ratcheted up the pressure, culminating with an offer to pay for Christopher's share to attend, which was not cheap, never cheap, when it came to these boys of La Salle. But F was doing well in Seattle—happily married, adorable twin girls aged nine, a systems engineer in Boeing's senior management—unlike Christopher, who hadn't ventured further than Macau, at least not for almost thirty years, who'd never finished university, but who still managed to scrape by thanks to his steady, dead-end job at home in Hong Kong.

They were all there, F and R and D and B and many others who were well established, a few socially prominent, sucking up champagne as they gazed out over Victoria Harbour, high up at the bar of the Upper House. Christopher had heard of but never been to this boutique hotel, this playground of those who had arrived. They were all there, these boys pushing fifty, laughing about the Maryknoll girls they had once lusted after, recalling old rivalries with the boys of DBS or Wah Yan, indulging in a shared past when life was still the promise of a bright future for those who survived the public exams and climbed the steps of secondary education in their crowd of elite 名校 "name schools" towards university. Christopher was only in touch with F now. R and D barely remembered him, and B nodded in recognition at the boy whose English homework he used to crib. Christopher Woo's English had always been good because his father was a judge, now long retired, and his mother… but that was the problem.

Christopher wandered away from F across the large, atrium-like space towards the hors d'oeuvres. His stomach was sour, unused as it was to champagne. A 35th year was no big deal, but this year coincided with "the 15th annual anniversary" of the handover of the city from Britain back to China in 1997. Christopher had laughed out loud at the redundancy. "Anniversaries *are* annual,"he emailed F, but his comment was ignored. Just as it would be here among the post-colonials, these neo-colonials of China. He picked up a menu from one of the tables, and there it was again: "15th annual anniversary." Christopher knew that language had been abandoned for more urgent pleasures. A 15th anniversary was not necessarily that big a deal, either, but this year also coincided with the changeover to the city's third chief executive since the return to China after British rule. That *was* a big deal because their former classmate, a boy who had not spoken to Christopher in the eleven years they were in school together, had been anointed to the inner circle of the new government, a member of the true, and overpaid, elite. So this was the Thursday before the ceremony Sunday, and their classmate could get drunk and have time to slough off his hangover before having to appear respectable again.

Christopher nibbled on a caviar tart. His jacket sleeve hung a tad too long and was slightly smeared with horserad-ish from the smoked fish savory he'd scooped up. He dabbed at the sleeve with a paper napkin, which made the stain worse. Only a drycleaner could fix it now. But he knew F wouldn't mind, the way F never seemed to mind about anything. They had become friends-for-life at nine when F beat up an older boy who circled Christopher with a bully brigade at recess in the toilet. F told him, "Don't be afraid. I'll take care of you," and each year when F made the pilgrimage home to visit his parents, he called Christopher, hung out with him for a few evenings, and listened to him talk about his life before flying back to his own in Seattle. He was the only one of Chris-topher's social media milieu who wrote him in English, not Chinese, and who lived the kind of life Christopher knew he should live but couldn't. They were even Facebook friends.

He could almost wear F's suit jackets and shirts, which was odd because F was taller but had a short torso and long legs while Christopher had a long upper body and slightly shorter arms. All of F's clothes were tailored, just as Christo-pher's father had a tailored wardrobe. Father had liked F a lot, and Mother did, too, back when his family lived together in the big house on Flint Road—walking distance to La Salle—where F liked to hang out with him after school and where, on Thursdays, they spied upon girls through his father's binoculars, watched them in their butt-revealing ballet tunics at the dance school across the road. Christopher didn't want to have to think about Mother anymore now that she was dead.

F came by the hors d'oeuvres table asking, "So what do you think of this?", meaning the city's new Chief Executive. F was sociable and successful, but he didn't always think highly of all their former classmates which was why, Christopher assumed, they were still friends. F kept on talking—wasn't this view amazing, didn't B look fit, how did Christopher like that caviar tart—until his eyes landed on the stained sleeve and he paused. Christopher thought he looked annoyed, but that passed and then he was just F again, talking about his daughters who were taking ballet—one was good and the other had duck feet. They both laughed over Duck Lake, which had been F's sister's favorite joke, the younger sister who'd married a Frenchman, lived in Tokyo now, and worked for an international bank, the former Maryknoll girl Christopher had given his heart to until F had to tell him, "Stop. She's just not interested." That had ended Christopher's teenaged love life; he hadn't met anyone since who compared, which was what he told F whenever F asked if he was seeing anyone.

B joined them at the table, and from their conversation Christopher was surprised to find that F and B had been in touch a lot more over the years than he knew. B worked for a major developer now and made a lot of money; he'd come a long way from the resettled refugee life of his youth in public housing. La Salle used to be like that, education for all even though it was a 名校, government-funded. The Catholics were like that. Now, B's parents lived in a luxury flat, paid for entirely by B. Christopher hadn't even known that F knew B's family, or that they'd hung out back in school. All he knew was that B's English had been lousy but he'd aced Chinese, which hadn't been Christopher's good subject, and they'd tutored each other, cribbing each other's notes to get through the exams. Mother only spoke to him in impeccable Queen's English. B was saying to F, "My mother has arthritis, but I suppose that's normal when you get older," and F was telling him about his mother's acid reflux and how he'd told her to stop eating so much, and they both laughed. Christopher was still nibbling on the caviar tart.

"Are you ever going to finish that?" B asked before wandering off to join another group.

At dinner, Christopher sat next to F. The butter knife, soup spoon, fish and meat knives and forks, and dessert spoon and fork were all correctly placed, the way he knew silverware should be laid. His mother was Eurasian and had insisted on laying both an English and Chinese table correctly, and she'd made sure Christopher learned.

"I went by your old house yesterday," F told him. "It's a school now."

Christopher was surprised. He hadn't been anywhere near the house for at least two decades, if not longer. At first, after his parents split up, he had gone by all the time, until F told him, "Stop. Forget about it," agreeing that Christopher's father's behavior was "unconscionable." Christopher had liked that word, *unconscionable*. It accurately described the cause of his mother's plight, even though Mother was, of course, mad, crazy, completely off her rocker. By the time Father had made the affair with Dr. Cheung's sister public and left them, abandoning him to the nothingness of life with Mother, it was an open secret that she was nuts. He had only been sixteen then but couldn't abandon Mother. She clung to him ferociously in any case, said he owed his life to her. Her family wouldn't help; they had long ago disinherited her. They were all crazy, too, in any case: she and her four sisters all extravagantly spending the last of their grandfather's wealth on designer clothes and shoes and bags instead of jewelry that they could at least have pawned. The one surviving maternal aunt had wandered the streets of Tsim Sha Tsui, homeless. When Christopher occasionally sighted her, he gave her cash, but she was the *completely* loony one, beyond all hope.

The Flint Road home had belonged to Father's family. Father took what jewelry there was, along with Mother's Hongkong and Shanghai Bank shares, "for the medical bills," he said. When Mother's skin condition first erupted at the age of twelve—*like leprosy*, he'd told F at the time, even though it wasn't—Dr. Cheung, who lived two houses down, had treated her. She got better, but kept buying things, once spending two months of Father's salary in one afternoon on ball gowns and ten pairs of evening shoes. His parents had fought late into the early morning when Mother ran out to the driveway in nothing but her underwear. Only her amah's urging got her back inside. Mother's personal amah from girlhood, who died soon afterward from old age and a broken heart over Mother.

Father had given Christopher a choice: "Leave her. She belongs in Castle Peak," meaning the insane asylum, but Christopher didn't think his mother was *that* crazy and didn't want to see her shut away. Then Dr. Cheung's sister, the nice Chinese (not Eurasian) girl from Maryknoll finally succumbed to Father's urgings and had an affair with him so that Father could leave Mother, and him, to their fates. Christopher knew perfectly well that he did not live up to Father's standards academically or otherwise and probably never would. Once, maybe ten years or so after the abandonment, when Christopher had failed for the third time to finish a university degree despite stints at one British and two American schools, his father had said, "You'll never amount to anything" and finally given up on him for good.

"So what do you think of our new CE?" F was saying. "You followed the election, right?"

Of course he had, he told F. How could he not, given his 24/7 media access, monitoring both print and electronic news, the one perk of his long-time job at the clipping service? How quaint that sounded. It had been a long time since he'd needed to "clip" a story out of a newspaper the way he used to for this international PR company that had kept him on—*had it really been twenty-five years already?*—because his English was fluent and he was literate in Chinese and could write research report summaries for their clients overseas from his back-room office or his computer at home. He wanted to tell F everything he had been thinking about the two contenders for the CE post—well, three really, but no one ever thought the third had a hope in hell—who'd blundered their way through an "election campaign" of teacup-storm proportions, but he didn't know how to say it. Christopher didn't even know what to say as F talked about his old home, the house he had loved so much as a child, with its high walls and second-floor bed-room where he could spy on the girls at ballet school across the road in the afternoon and dream in bed at night about F's sister, the girl who gave him all those wet dreams he couldn't tell F about. What did it matter, these silly scandals the loser in this election was embroiled in, illegal structures in his home and revelations about some affair with an aide? Christopher knew from the time he was a boy that the affairs of state didn't matter. What mattered was what you had for breakfast and dinner and whether the table settings were correct for a Chinese or English banquet.

Now, he gazed down at the silverware. Its expensive so-lidity provided an artful accent to this Upper House where, for a night, he was back where he belonged. With F and that life of the school they'd attended as boys, the school Father had attended as a boy and where Christopher's son would have attended had he had an heir. It was succession, this life of the elite, unless your mother went crazy and believed her skin condition was due to the poison fed her by her rival, Dr. Cheung's unmarried sister, who, when she visited her broth-er, was always elegantly dressed with just the right jewelry to accent her pure Chinese skin, skin that wasn't mottled with a leprosy-like ailment in which layers peeled off and the white of her cheeks were like those of a Chinese ghost. The soup arrived—wild mushroom—and Christopher wondered if mushrooms were ever tame although he didn't dare say this to F. He would have once, when F had laughed at all his jokes, but he suspected that these days F wouldn't laugh anymore. They weren't gay, he and F, although Christopher had wondered briefly about it because what he felt for F was nothing short of love, the way he loved all of F's family, who had always been nice to him. Even the sister would smile sweetly and say nice things if she happened to be around, and F's parents would politely ask after his mother even though they knew she was crazy. He thought of them as his protectors the way F had been all those years ago in the playground. Some things didn't change even though F had looked a little askance earlier at the smudged sleeve. Christopher almost said he would get it cleaned but remained mute, unable to say a word in the light of F's momentary, disapproving glare. But he was imagining. It wasn't a glare—it wasn't. F wasn't Father, who summoned up the judgment of a vengeful god when he glared at his son, this useless failure, this almost dead ringer for the wife he never forgave himself for marrying, this final scab that advertised his own loss of face, first as a husband, then as a father. F wasn't Father, the man who couldn't love back, despite all the love Christopher had surrendered to him. F wasn't Father, the coward who ran away. F was his friend for life and always would be.

The soup was too thin, rendering the mushroom flavor overly strong; of this much Christopher was sure. Just as he hadn't lost his ability to intuit when change was in the air, or when something was wrong, you didn't lose taste once it was bred into you, despite the years of neglect in between. Christopher had watched as Father headed towards the abandonment, struggling nightly to hold onto family, to do the right thing. Father should have understood that once you took the road less traveled, as he had with Mother, you couldn't turn back with impunity. Like F with him. Their annual reunions were always exclusive evenings alone together, well, really, *evening*, singular, in the last few years. One day it had hit him that whenever F visited now they never spent more than one evening alone, and hardly ever with F's wife or girls the way they used to when F and his wife were newly married.

Luckily F didn't ask him about the soup, and then the fish arrived, a choice of skate or rainbow trout, neither one seen that often on Hong Kong menus, although Christopher wouldn't have known. What he recalled was the taste of trout from the faraway time when Father still believed in him. Even Dr. Cheung's sister had believed in him, at least for awhile, and she had, or so Christopher suspected, defended him to Father once she became the wife, usurping Mother's place officially so that she no longer had to blush in shame over her condition as a mistress and almost-spinster. Dr. Cheung's sister wasn't especially beautiful—certainly Mother in her day had been ten times lovelier—but she was educated and accomplished and a respectable member of society, the principal of the primary section at Maryknoll. She did not expect her husband to indulge unreasonable demands or the vicissitudes of a spoilt childhood among the formerly rich and famous, like Mother, who floated through life on the kind of beauty and glamour that makes the social pages for a brief, forgettable time. How Father must have been smitten with her! It had to be adoration, if not love, for him to defy his family and marry a woman who was half Chinese. Christopher chose the rainbow trout but was disappointed to find mere slices, deboned and topped by some fancy sauce in the guise of nouveau cuisine, instead of a whole fish.

F had taken him trout fishing once. This was when Christopher was still trying to finish a bachelor's degree at a university somewhere. Theatre. Literature. Even philosophy. He tried one course in world religion but fell asleep in the middle of a midterm exam while writing about the life of the Buddha. He dropped the class. During the semester break he and F had camped out by a lake and cooked trout over an open fire. That was living. That was something to write home about, not that he ever wrote home, not even to answer Mother's weekly, later daily, letters begging him to come home, saying that Father beat her, starved her, while *that woman* poisoned her tea with arsenic. He didn't respond. Later, she told him she was virtually penniless, that all she had to eat each day was rice gruel because Father was threatening to cut off her money. On and on it went until he finally came home for good and forgot about the life he was supposed to live, telling himself that he would go back to school later. He took one clerical job after another to earn the rent because by then, Father really *had* cut off the money. Dr. Cheung's sister found him jobs. She was like that, compassionate if not beautiful, and a school principal knew a lot of people.

F was eating the skate. "This is delicious," he said, but the butterflied corpse looked like a mutant squid to Christopher. The boys of La Salle were chattering loudly about the new CE, a man with initials in his name. They all had initials. It was no longer fashionable to use Anglo names: many of the non-Catholic boys had dropped the Bartholomews and Gabriels and Abrahams, these misnomers that had sounded grand to teenaged ears when being quasi-Anglo was the respectable, elitist thing to be. Now they were Y.Y. or M.B. or M.G.M. and quasi-fluent in Mandarin for all Christopher knew since he didn't know anyone other than the three standing next to F.

Now, the red queen took over as an undoubtedly expensive, decanted red made its way around the tables while waiters hurried to change plates and pour the right wine for the steak that would follow. The steak, Christopher thought, was marching its way out of the kitchen like a brigade of tin soldiers. He was feeling a bodily heat and a little giddy from the white wine and champagne. Did they always eat and drink like this, these classmates who were no longer, who never had been, his friends? F had told the waiter, "He likes his medium rare," and there it was, the succulent flesh of cattle, flanked by asparagus spears and Brussels sprouts. Brussels sprouts, like on *Leave It To Beaver* that he'd watched as a boy with Mother, afterward asking her to please, please make him Brussels sprouts because he was curious to try this exotically named vegetable. She found frozen ones at Dairy Lane, the fancy supermarket next to Lane Crawford's in Tsim Sha Tsui. How was it he could recall the minutiae of life before Mother went mad but couldn't remember what he ate for breakfast? Christopher stared at the steak, almost afraid to taste it.

"Aren't you hungry?" F asked, and Christopher was startled. It suddenly seemed to him that F was really asking, "Aren't you grateful for this seat at my table?" No, he told himself, that wasn't it. F wasn't Father, who banished him forever from his table. F wasn't crazy like Mother, who died last

Christmas, simply keeled over at the dinner table and expired. Christopher had sat, dumbstruck, until the smell of fecal matter spurred him into action. The arrangements! He had saved money for a proper Catholic funeral the way she'd insisted, promising her he *wouldn't* dump her body without ceremony, promising her he *would* publish a proper obituary in the *South China Morning Post,* as befitted her stature and fine family origins, so that her world could mourn her passing. He was true to his word. No one came to the funeral, not even Father. Only F sent flowers.

The boys of La Salle were toasting their classmate, the one who had never spoken a single word to Christopher in school and who hadn't said a word to him this evening, either. They rose in unison to honor him. Christopher wanted to remain seated. F nudged him to stand, which he did, reluctantly, not wanting to be rude to F. The whole room was like a stage, all of them play-acting some drama that had nothing to do with Christopher's real life. They were all here to keep the drama in motion, glad-handing handshakes and utterances that paved the way for themselves and their heirs. They were all here for the 15th annual anniversary and the 3rd ascension, dressed in their tailored and designer suits, their highly polished calf-leather shoes, slipped on over socks that would be replaced when worn, not darned like Christopher's with a meticulous precision that would have startled and perhaps even pleased Father had he known, the kind of precision Father's excellent mind was capable of as he sat in judgment of everyone in this top-heavy city that was sinking under its own weight, where the sun rose in a reddish, reddened east, backlit from up north in Beijing. Christopher wanted to tell F that one day they would all be gone and another slate of boys would take their places, would try to keep their footing at the top of the hill where they now rose in unison for a military song of historical long-march struggles they had never known or wanted to know.

F nudged him to sit, because Christopher was the last one standing after the toast. The glances of pity by R, D, and B were not lost on Christopher as he slid back down, nor on F, he couldn't help noticing. No, not F. F did not pity him. Never. Dr. Cheung's sister, now that was pity. Father said she had *empathy* for the less fortunate students who were in her charge. But Christopher knew, when it came to him, that all she felt was that distant cousin, sympathy, pity's honorable twin.

The knife slid through the steak. *Slid*. It was soft and juicy and overwhelmingly large, but Christopher ate it all, surprised that so much food fit inside him at one sitting. "You need to eat more," F had said a few years earlier, shocked by how emaciated he looked. Christopher had shrugged and said it was nothing, only hard work caring for Mother as she aged, as physical ailments exacerbated her mental state. That was the year F had come to his home to visit him and Mother, when Christopher could see that F had had no idea how deteriorated Mother was, how the daily grind was truly that. F simply couldn't know because he lived a life without a mother going crazy and a father who stopped loving you one day and never found it in his heart to love you ever again.

Christopher had called F to tell him about his mother's passing, the only person he bothered to tell. His daily life was so far removed from F's and the world he had once known so why bother saying much? Really, why? You lived, that was all, and one day Mother was gone and life went on as usual. You went to work each morning, scanned the news that was fit to clip for your company's clients, drank tea with your colleagues, who told you about their lives and complained about the Gini coefficient of Hong Kong where the rich pretended to be middle class in order not to suffer guilt at being so very, very privileged, while the sea of poverty rose around them, an angry tide swelling into a tsunami. And then one day it was the 35th reunion that coincided with the 15th annual anniversary of the penultimate handover of your city's past and you wondered if you should go and then here you were. Right here. Now. Watching regret invade F, perhaps even more than regret, shame over you, the inappropriate friend. Forcing out Mother, who stubbornly resisted oblivion. Indulging in but not savoring this divine meal. Divining Father, who forced you towards Lethe, as if your very existence were his to deny. Dreading the day when F no longer responded to your calls or texts or emails. Un-friended you. Here you were. Right now. Waiting for the fall.

THE LOAN

for Wilma & Merly, my 妹妹

CHAN **Lai-tai tugged at her skirt belt as she readied herself for work.** No way to cinch it tighter. Should losing only five pounds make such a difference?

Xiong would repay her today. He had brought it up this morning, the only thing he said after kissing her, just before dashing out to catch the early train to Guangzhou. Never time to make love when he was in a hurry. Did he remember his keys? He'd left a set in Guangzhou last trip, and she'd had to scramble to make him a new one. So forgetful! But that wasn't important because something else nagged. What? Something at work? Her boss, Mrs. Lung, was playing catch-up after her trip to Thailand. Which meant, as usual, that too much work got piled onto Lai-tai.

As she headed towards the MTR, she felt in her jacket pocket for the ticket. Its magnetic stripe caressed her finger, reassuring that yes, Xiong *could* remember if he chose to do so. All it took was a row—and it had been nasty, loud, her slamming the door on the way out—when she accused him of taking her tickets because he couldn't keep track of his own, and worse, not telling her, causing her unnecessary stress and embarrassment when she stood at the barrier searching for her ticket, holding up the line behind her.

Or had he simply not found this one in her jacket?

The MTR hum momentarily stilled her own and Ma's unrelenting voices. *Did I work so hard after leaving China just so my daughter would be worse off than a prostitute? At least a prostitute only sacrifices her body.* Her mother, a first wife, walked out on Lai-tai's father some thirty years earlier after he'd married a *siu tai-tai* in the late sixties, back when concubine marriages were still legal. She later refused to ever let him meet Lai-tai, with whom she had been pregnant at the time. Ma was apoplectic when she first learned that Xiong already had a wife and family in Guangzhou. Now, over two years since Lai-tai first got together with Xiong, she thought it was clear he really loved her and couldn't do without her. Yet Ma wouldn't relent. *Stupid girl, you're young, only twenty-nine. Intelligent and pretty, a good figure except when you don't eat enough and lose too much weight. Don't do this to yourself. Don't waste your life.*

Didn't his love count for anything?

She arrived early at work but already, Mrs. Lung was there. If only she could beat the old dragon into the office! Just once. After four years, Lai-tai had almost quit trying.

Her boss glanced up at her as she settled at her desk. "Oh, so early. Yang Xiong must be in Guangzhou, hah? She always used his full name, assigning him a distinct, yet somehow tenuous, reality.

"Only for the day. He's back tonight."

"Oh yeah?" But she left it at that.

Lai-tai tried to ignore the unspoken jibe, that Xiong knew

where his dick slept best. Her boss could be crude. *Fei Loong Pao who'd sleep with you?* All the staff called their boss "fatty dragon dumpling" behind her back, the homonymic pun on her name being too irresistible. She was just jealous. Lai-tai tried to imagine that mass of middle-aged womanhood having sex with her hen-pecked, emaciated husband. Grotesque. She set about her day's work. It bugged her how everyone exaggerated her "situation." Even her older sister, Lai-li, who usually was an ally against Ma, derided her. *It's already 1998. Don't you know concubines are unfashionable now? They belong in the mainland, not here! Besides, for all his big talk about business and Guangzhou "connections," he's just another* "big six bumpkin" *struggling to send money back home.* Lai-li was too mercenary and insensitive for her own good, which was why, at over thirty, she was *still* without either a husband or regular boyfriend. Probably jealous, Lai-li having once had designs of her own on Xiong before she found out he was married. Lai-tai hadn't told her about the loan, afraid of her censorious laughter. Her sister simply no longer had proper feelings.

Her sister would laugh even more if she knew how much Xiong actually expressed concern for her. He said Lai-li, who managed sales for a very successful Chinese electronics manufacturer in Shenzhen, needed a less stressful job. It was true her sister worked extremely long hours. Between business trips to China and Europe as well as all the entertainment of buyers in the evenings, she hardly had time for herself. But when Xiong recently suggested Lai-li should come work for him, she angrily squelched that idea. If he needed a loan to keep his business going then the *last* thing he could afford was to employ her sister who made very good money at her job. They had fought over that. Bitterly. She hated it when he condescended because he was twelve years her senior, saying she didn't understand how business worked, because after all, her work experience was only in companies with limited potential. He had *vision*. He was trying to expand internationally, to Europe and even America, unlike Fei Loong Pao's small trading company which only sold trinkets around Asia. It was so unfair! He had no real idea what her employer did, how she sourced and produced promotional items for large Asian companies, because she knew many purchasing and procurement managers. Lai-tai knew how profitable the company was, unlike Xiong's business. His failing business.

At around a quarter to one, just before lunch, Xiong called, surprising her. Peter, the IT guy from shipping, was standing by her desk, but she signaled for him to come back later. "Don't tell me," she began. "You have to stay the night, don't you?" This had been the case the last three trips, always with some "urgent" excuse that sounded fake.

"Why do you always think the worst? I said I was coming back and I am."

The hurt in his voice got her the way it always did. "I'm sorry." *Another* apology, even though she told herself she would stop apologizing to him. Yet somehow, he'd done it again, made it seem entirely her fault.

"I just need your help."

She bristled. "What is it this time?"

"Calm down, it's for a very dear family friend, Yin-fei. You know, the one who's almost like a sister to me? She was in Hong Kong a few months ago trying to apply for a job and stayed with us? She's so smart, she'll get one eventually. Anyway, she's quite ill, badly needs to see a doctor in Hong Kong. It might be something serious and you know how hopeless the hospitals here are. But you know how it is, she didn't get her exit permit till today, so that's why it's all last minute. I'm so sorry about this, and she'd also apologize for the inconvenience, for sure. Obviously she can't travel by herself, so it's best if she comes with me. We're taking the five o'clock."

Another drama rationally explained. So perfectly understandable that he did not even have to justify his unspoken demand—that she should erase her presence in *their* home by the time he got back and stay elsewhere, her mother's most likely, until Yin-fei left. A huge inconvenience, especially right now when work was so busy, and an imposition on Ma. An unreasonable, worse, *hypocritical* demand, to pretend that Yin-fei was staying with "us." She flinched in anticipation of Ma's harangue which would inevitably happen and wondered if she could crash with Lai-li instead.

"Listen, must go, I'm going to be cut off."

"Xiong, wait…" but the line went dead. Damned payphones. Of course, he couldn't call from his home, not with his wife hovering, as Xiong said she did.

Lai-tai knew also that she would have to leave the office too early just to hurry home, incurring Fei Loong Pao's wrath.

"Hey birthday girl, are you coming or not? You'll lose us our table. We're only generous once a year." Maria Tang's voice, a tad too shrill, assailed her from across the office. She managed shipping, where all the staff operated in perpetual panic, scrambling to fulfill orders and mollify customers because their Shenzhen supplier was, predictably, late again.

"I'm coming, I'm coming." Lai-tai grabbed her purse and ran to catch up with the group as they headed towards their usual restaurant.

At lunch, the bamboo steamers of dim sum piled to an all-time high. Lai-tai picked at her food, saying little. She barely registered the raucous laughter and conversation, and it wasn't till Maria nudged her, saying "Wei! Peter's talking to you," that she looked across the table at her colleague.

"Ms. Chan, you're eating too little today." He was dividing up the platter of fried noodles into bowls, and had heaped an especially large one for her, complete with two juicy shrimps on top.

"Oh too much, too much," she protested as he passed it round to her. "I can't eat all that. One of the guys should take it."

Ah Chun stuck his hand out, but Peter slapped it back. "Don't be a hog, you. Come on," he coaxed, "six of you could fit into one Fei Loong Pao."

Everyone laughed. Ah Chun pulled a face. "Ahh, quit trying to sweet-talk her. She doesn't need your attention on her birthday when she has better prospects than you. After all, *Mrs.* Chan-Yang is already spoken for." He guffawed at his own joke.

Peter turned red, his crush on Lai-tai too publicly called out. An uneasy silence settled over the table. Maria shot Ah Chun a dirty look. "Talking rubbish again, aren't you? Shut that hog mouth!" He shrugged, unconcerned, took the offending bowl of noodles, and commenced eating.

Normally, Lai-tai would have dismissed his remark. Ah Chun was just being his usual blunt, clunky self. But today, instead of joining Maria's banter with a pointed comeback to make everyone laugh, she glared defiantly at her colleagues and declared, "A *siu tai-tai* is also a wife, you know."

No one said a word. Maria rolled her eyes then waved her chopsticks at everyone and blurted out, "Why all this yapping today? Come on, let's eat. Food's getting cold."

Lunch hastened towards its finale.

Back at the office, Maria tugged Lai-tai's sleeve just before they returned to their desks. "You can fire him, you know. He really crossed the line." As office manager, Lai-tai's power over the lower-level administrative staff was paramount. Ah Chun was lazy and sometimes rude to customers. But he had been with the company since its inception, and could be trusted with petty cash and the daily banking and knew where all the supplies in the closet were stacked. He even cleaned the toilets the time Fei Loong Pao forgot to renew the cleaning services contract and generally kept the kitchen clean. It would be impossible to hire a replacement who did his mix of jobs for the relatively low salary he was paid.

"Forget it, he didn't mean anything by it. And neither did I." She was about to say more but Maria's face, sympathetic yet slightly disdainful, stopped her short.

"Okay, whatever," Maria responded. "It's your face."

Embarrassed, Lai-tai returned to her desk. How she wished she hadn't said that and made a fool of herself in front of everyone.

The afternoon dragged. She tried to concentrate but everything distracted. Damn Ah Chun. And Maria. And even Peter, whom she wished would stop with his unrequited heart. After all, she had never encouraged him, never led him on. What did they all know, anyway? *It's all about love, nothing else really. Especially for a woman. Love is fundamental to a woman's nature, something you can't deny. You and I, we can't change our histories, our lives. But we need each other Lai-tai, we belong together. What we do is our business, no one else's.* In the intimacy of their love, through all the tears she couldn't squelch, she desperately hoped Xiong was right, especially when he gripped her buttocks in his large hands, possessing the moment, as if he never wanted to let her go.

Her thoughts returned to the loan. How long had it been? Three, no four months? More than four. Xiong hadn't exactly *asked* to borrow. In fact, how had it happened? Sick daughter, medical bills eating into savings, a run of bad luck with business partners who cheated him. At first, he cut back on expenses, performed nobly for her benefit. *I'll skip dinner tonight, I can't contribute my share to groceries.* Of course she dismissed that, told him not to be silly. Yes, it had begun like that, these remarks about economizing. Walking instead of taking a bus or taxi, not buying new underwear even though his were almost threadbare. At first she simply helped him out with these small expenses, and he would always be effusive in his gratitude, saying this was temporary which she assured him she knew. The sex that followed would be amazing, but soon all his protests began to feel like a kind of performance. Yet she vanquished such unkind thoughts—she *loved* him, didn't she?—but for now, she was paying all their utilities, the entire rent, and all day-to-day expenses and…

"Ms. Chan, did you hear me?" Peter had been standing by her desk for several minutes. "You were supposed to give me cash for the shipment today?"

She stared back blankly until it clicked. Of course! That was what she was supposed to do this morning. "Yes, sorry," she said, pretending to rummage in her desk drawer, knowing full well she hadn't prepared it. "I'll bring it round in a few minutes."

He didn't budge. "That's what you said yesterday. It's already four thirty."

Fuck! The bank was closed. And, she knew, Peter was supposed to go to Shenzhen early tomorrow morning, before the bank opened, to deliver the promised computer to their supplier and pick up that shipment of plaques for one of their largest customers, which was what he needed the cash for. He would catch hell from Fei Loong Pao if he didn't go. "How much was it again?" He told her. Lai-tai made a quick mental calculation, thinking she could perhaps cover it from her own account, which, unlike the company's account, she could access with her ATM card. She couldn't, not till after payday next week. If only… previously, she could have solved the problem easily enough, but that loan had depleted so much of her savings that she no longer had any contingency for larger amounts. Her face must have betrayed something, because Peter winced and backed away, saying, "Look, don't worry, I'll go the day after tomorrow, okay? But I really must by then. It is, uh, kinda urgent."

"I'm sorry, I'm sorry. I promise I'll take care of it first thing tomorrow. And I'll tell Fei Loong Pao it was my fault."

"Ms. Chan, it's no big deal. Forget about it. It was my own fault for not reminding you earlier." He paused, an uncertain look on his face. "You have a lot on your mind, for sure." He left quickly. The pity in his eyes shamed her.

She left work fifteen minutes later, much earlier than she should, having first acknowledged her mistake to Mrs. Lung who started with a tantrum but then softened. "Okay, fine, I forgive you, but only because it's your birthday. Go on home to your lover and tell him to take you somewhere nice for dinner. You're only young once." Peter's face haunted her as she left. Tomorrow, mustn't forget. It wasn't fair to cause her colleague such anxiety. All she needed was a clearer head and she would be fine. She could do that. She must. This determination lifted her mood as she headed towards the MTR.

In less than two hours, Xiong would be back with Yin-fei, and she would have cleaned up their home and eradicated her presence so that no one could actually tell a woman lived there. It was a trick she had mastered, easily accomplished without fuss, something Xiong said he loved her dearly for even as he apologized for the necessary deception, temporary, as he always repeated, only for old friends from Guangzhou who knew his family, the ones who couldn't possibly understand. Everyone in Hong Kong knew they were a couple. It was nothing, she told him, she could handle this minor inconvenience, and besides, guests who needed to stay had only come a few times, six or seven perhaps since they decided to live together a year and a half ago and moved into a flat and began to share their lives. *No one has ever loved me as much as you,* he would say, just before making her climax with such force that she would agree to anything afterward. Just like the loan that she'd offered one night in bed, a loan he accepted almost too quickly considering his loud protests (*I really shouldn't, you really mustn't, I feel so bad about this, it's just a temporary bridge loan*), a loan he promised fervently to repay within a month, with interest. He even signed an I.O.U. right away, getting out of bed naked to write it, to prove his sincerity. When a month passed, and nothing happened, she hadn't said anything at first, thinking, *any day now, it's just a question of timing, for sure. Cash flow in business is like that.* After the second month, she lodged a gentle reminder, and he had been so sad and apologetic, bowing to her, saying how embarrassed he was but things were still difficult although he knew that was no excuse and how terrible he felt. His humbling himself so shamed her that she dropped the subject completely. Then the promises, always unexpected, that he would manage something that day. The day would pass and nothing. The days and weeks passed, until the loan became this thing, unspoken, that hung between them.

But today was different. Even though he hadn't remembered her birthday, there was something in his voice this morning. Lai-tai was sure of it. Everything would be resolved after Yin-fei left. She recalled the photo he showed her several months earlier, before the loan, before Yin-fei's last visit which had also been a last minute scramble for Lai-tai to move out for... it had been four nights that time. Xiong did say when he called earlier this trip might be a little longer, a week or so. In the photo, Xiong and Yin-fei were standing under a tree in their swimsuits at a beach and he had his arm around her. An attractive woman, a year younger than him, whom he'd known since high school. *My wife's so jealous of her, isn't that silly, there's really never been anything between us, we're just very close friends* and Lai-tai had swelled with pride, thinking how much better a wife *she* was to him, how much real trust there was between them, the way a marriage should be. One day, he *would* find a way, as he promised, to divorce his wife and marry her. They could even buy the flat they were renting, and it would become their home and then maybe they could finally have a child. How badly she wanted that. One day, one day. *Patience, it will happen*, Xiong promised.

The journey home was zipping along, and felt much quicker than her morning's commute. It was a long ride from the office in Kowloon Bay back home to Sai Wan Ho on the island side, which was another contentious issue about Xiong for Ma. *Why does he want you to move so far away? What's wrong with Kwun Tong? It's much closer to your job.* She thought Lai-tai didn't want to be near her anymore, because she had raised both girls in her tiny Kwun Tong flat. But that wasn't true. Ma didn't understand how important it was for Xiong to be at a more prestigious address, for his business image. She had tried to explain but Ma simply wouldn't listen, comparing her to Lai-li who bought a flat close by, complaining, *and why so much money on decoration? You could have put a down payment on a flat instead and owned a home by now. I would have helped you, you know that.* It was different for her sister though. She made a lot more money, and she wasn't in love.

A strange relief overtook her. Xiong had said of Yin-fei—she was kind and sweet and trusting like Lai-tai, which was why he loved her, adding, *but only like a sister of course.* She even told Lai-li the first time Yin-fei stayed over and she crashed at her sister's so as not to suffer Ma's recriminations, saying, *he's so loyal to his close friends it really speaks well of his character,* but Lai-li said *ahhh you're naïve, he's probably fucking her,* and she, horrified, protested, *don't say that you just don't know him, he's honest and faithful to me. You just don't know how to trust anyone.* Her sister sniffed, saying, *how can you talk about fidelity when he has a wife?*

The hum of the MTR was eerily quiet. In fifteen minutes or so, she would be home. Xiong would have some if not all of the money to repay her. She knew he would. He said so and somehow she knew, this time, it *would* happen. As the train pulled into her station, she also hoped Yin-fei wouldn't need to stay too long once her visit to the doctor's was over.

THE TRANSUBSTANTIATION
OF THE ANTS

ALONE photographer captured the funnel of winged beauties. Thousands of nymphalids, a color tornado, ascending up and out to sea, away from Hong Kong towards Bermuda. He, the photographer, was in a helicopter early that morning, too early, when only the moon lit the sky. The previous night's downpour had cleared the air, and in that moment, a visual image to be recalled on his deathbed.

Months earlier, the white-yellow ants had begun planning their migration, preparing themselves for the eve of the great escape.

"But we have no blood!" the queen exclaimed, not for the first time. The colony's workers scurried food towards her, trying to calm their over-excitable monarch. Nearby, a black and blue butterfly hovered over a dead rat, blood oozing from its neck where a dog had bitten deep and hard before flinging it away.

"She looks like she's going to a ball," whispered Gala, a young ant, as she gazed, fascinated, at the blood and butterfly.

"How do you know it's a girl?" her best friend Cripps Pink whispered back.

"Because she *must* be."

That night, Prince Consortium the winged drone stood proudly by his queen, as Sir Morphinae, the oldest flying ant, repeated the story that excited the younger ants.

"Our little colony was born in Hong Kong on a flap year, June 31, 1841. Unlike the Gregorian calendar, our calendar flaps instead of leaps, and is ruled by the breezes of butterfly wings. Our first queen was cursed at birth, having fallen into a pool of blood of a dying wild boar. This kept her in a state of permanent lethargy. Legend is that she considered herself more than an ant, and thought herself a blooded creature which ants of course are not. As long as she lived, Queen Nymphiadiant insisted on being constantly pregnant to prove that she would eventually give birth to a superior species. All the winged drones sacrificed themselves to her stubborn quest. In time, the colony shrank, and our ancestors mated with other colonies to survive, and we evolved into this white-yellow species of today. For over a century, our first queen was considered mad."

And here all the youngest ants piped up in unison: "Until, until, the birth of the Fragrant White Bauhinia, our Daddy Dwarf Tree!"

"And," said Gala, the most precocious, "the wild boars returned to the hills of the New Territories!"

Cripps Pink nudged her friend, trying to calm her down.

Gala was undaunted. "Please Sir Morphinae, isn't it almost time? We are at flap year again now at last, aren't we?"

Sir Morphinae smiled. "Yes, Gala, indeed we are, but you're getting ahead of things. What do we always say about our Grand Narrative?"

Once again the youngest ants chorused their response: "After the beginning and before the end, there must be a strong core, the well-constructed middle!"

Their nervous queen finally interrupted. "Enough, it's almost midnight."

Despite the downpour earlier that evening, hope in the colony was palpable. All gathered on the branches of their Daddy Dwarf Bauhinia, waiting. As foretold, it was in full bloom and the scent intoxicated. A sharpened branch, fashioned after years of patient work by the colony, stood in wait. Soon the wild boar would arrive, and the prophecy would come to pass.

At the first stroke of midnight, a distant rumbling. It got louder at the second stroke. By the third stroke, Sir Morphinae breathed a sigh of relief. Here it was, the mad racing boar to free them forever, to revise the history of Queen Nymphiadiant's madness.

In the distance, the night sky was aflame as the British departed the city of Hong Kong.

The boar somersaulted in the air and *splat!* Impaled on the sharpened branch. His blood oozed. The colony swarmed towards the viscous crimson, plunged in, and drank.

Gala shrieked first: "It's happening!" The ants watched amazed as her wings burst forth and up she whirled in a frenetic dance. Soon all the other girl ants had transformed, and the winged drones came for them, swooping down in ecstasy to mate to their death. There was no one to witness this fluttering frenzy in the fragrance of Bauhinia. Han purple, red-violet, electric purple. Banana, lemon, bumblebee. Greens, oranges, midnight blues. All the colors that had never graced these white-yellow beings.

And then they flew off, this panoply of transubstantiated butterflies, having bathed in and drunk their fill of boar's blood. They left Hong Kong forever and headed to their new garden, verdant in Bermuda.

Only one photograph, shot just before dawn on June 31, 1997, was evidence of their glorious migration.

in other realms

HERE I AM

for P.K. Leung 梁秉鈞 [Ye Si 也斯] *in memoriam*

H E was not a zombie. Nor was he a ghoul, mummy, wraith, ambulatory skeleton or operatic phantom. He wasn't even *geong si,* a dressed-to-the-nines Qing dynasty vampire that could at least do an approximation of the Lindy Hop, transcending time and culture into the Jazz Age. However, he was clearly dead, or undead if you parsed language to its core.

Jonnie Tang sauntered down the pathway of Southorn Playground, skirted the border of the court, waiting to be seen. His real name was Tang Chun-ying, or CY, but a little over a year ago, he had started going by Jonnie, not wanting to be ragged on for his English initials that were the same as the city's Chief Executive. At least he used to be Jonnie Tang until 0555 hours. The idiot driver of that Bimmer M3 barreling east on Hennessy, along the north border of the playground, had run the light and slammed into him. Asshole didn't even have the balls to stop.

The force of impact had flung him into the plate glass window of the second-floor hair salon above the Circle K. Shattering glass severed his vocal cords, and a large, jagged, blade-like shard almost decapitated him. Not a desirable angle of repose, to be unrecognizably swathed on a gurney, smeared in blood and fecal matter, like a chicken with its head chopped off. Even the emergency team paled. He was gruesome.

Next thing you knew, Jonnie was the corpse on TVB Jade's evening news, being too late for the morning news at 6:30.

He could imagine his mother *tsk*-ing away at the radio news report later that morning. *Those reckless* 有錢 *boys and their cars! Hate to death those* have-money *brats. They should be locked up and forced to clean public toilets as community service!* His mother was *tsk*-ing about something else on the news, until the call came from the police, *are you the family of Tang Chun-ying?* Ma, he called across what he presumed to be an ethereal, omniscient panorama, I'm here, but his voice box was gone. He couldn't even say before he disappeared that this wasn't her fault, that she shouldn't blame herself as he knew she would.

Except that he hadn't disappeared, not really.

At Southorn, the gang was all there, waiting for him, calling out his mother's cunt at his tardiness. It was a little past 6:30 a.m., their appointed time to shoot hoops each Tuesday morning, a ritual observed for the last five years.

Hey, he yelled at the gang, here I am. King-wah was dribbling the ball in a slow dance. Jonnie tried, but could not step over the painted white line on the ground that bordered the court. What was this weirdness of being, voiceless, invisible, movement-impaired? Uncertain of his new existence, other than the certainty that he was dead, he avoided touching or bumping into solid objects, afraid that he could not pass through them (or was he actually afraid that he *could*?). Would he disintegrate when the sun rose, assuming it wasn't another rain-soaked morning? Did weather delay eternity?

King-wah loped near the border. Jonnie could almost touch him he was so close. *Where do you suppose he is*, King-wah was saying. *He wok-sapped me three, four hours ago, out dancing again, maybe he overslept?* The others laughed. *Dancing iron monkey king*, they named him, honoring the birth-year sign they all shared when metal reigned. *Hey*, said Yuk-sing, the disciplined one, *you know him, better late than on time.*

Fuck you, Yuk-sing, you sanctimonious jerk, Jonnie shouted. No sound emerged. In the distance, voices of the dead conversed, quarreled, hawked goods and services from a century ago. They confabbed further south, along what used to be the shoreline, long before Southorn Playground was borrowed from the sea in what became perpetual reclamation for the city's waterfront. So there *was* sound in this world, Jonnie realized. Someone was singing a Teresa Tang tune, that one with the English and Mandarin refrain *goodbye my love, wo de ai ren zai jian.*

King-wah moved away from him. Hey, Jonnie tried to say. Wait. Here I am! Talk to me please. I'm here, I'm here.

By evening, he assumed the gang would all have heard what happened, but Jonnie was still wandering around Wan Chai. It was unbearably crowded. If death was an eternity-populated Hong Kong, then he had to find a way out. What puzzled him was why he could smell such a lot of life, the stench of the waterfront, the cooking steam of the *dai pai dongs*, the pervasive odor of manure. Also, time disoriented. For one thing, he could see the waterfront, right where Southorn Playground used to be. Which meant he must be traveling backward in time to before reclamation. That was when it hit him, why the gang hadn't been able to hear him. It was the wrong Tuesday morning. No trace of the accident that almost decapitated him was evident; and so soon afterward, there should still have been debris and the blue wooden markers the police used to cordon off a crime scene. As he had flown upwards to his death, the sound of a falling something clanged against the roadway—perhaps a piece of the vehicle, dislodged from impact? Jonnie hadn't seen it but now the *ko-ling k-lang* replayed in his auditory recall. Also, King-wah had said something about *wok-sapping* him a few hours earlier and he knew for a fact that there had been no WhatsApp message on his phone the morning of his death. So it must have been another Tuesday, earlier, when he also hadn't shown up.

Okay, this was bullshit! he wanted to shriek. He had never imagined death—not that he had spent much time contemplating not being alive—to be so fraught with life and movement and people. Everyone seemed to be just going about their own business, regardless of their moment of time. The only advantage was that no one appeared to bump into anyone else, presumably because they were bodiless. Nothing made sense. He stood still, trying to calm himself and figure out what to do next.

A young girl, around fifteen or so, dressed in a short skirt that showed off her skinny, shapely legs, was moving towards him. She seemed headed directly for him, and Jonnie didn't know whether to move aside or acknowledge her or what?

Should he say, *hey I'm here watch where you're going*, because she appeared not to see him. She looked familiar, like he'd just seen her face somewhere. As she neared, he saw that she was in her school uniform, but that the left half of her was scrunched and scarred. The closer she came, the more unnerving she was. But Jonnie stood his ground. Then, she stopped right in front on him and shouted 你不是! and carried on—floating or walking, he couldn't be sure—and passed him by or, perhaps, slid right through him. What did she mean by that cry, *you-are-not!* And why in formal Chinese? It made no sense. Of course, nothing was making sense the longer he was dead.

Across Des Voeux Road at a street corner, he sighted a newspaper vendor. Jonnie traversed Des Voeux, noting that the trams were running, hoping he could strike up a conversation since vendors usually would speak to you, especially the women. Or at least they did among the living. *Apple Daily*, he said, digging into his pocket for coins, surprised to find he could hand these over to the vendor. And there she was, the girl who had just passed by, on the front page of the daily news, the suicide jumper from the top of Central Plaza a few blocks north, close to the waterfront. The date was a month or so earlier, right after exam results were released, when suicides were normal.

The woman vendor noted his interest, said, these *liangs* don't know how good they've got it to be able to go to school. At least they get a shot at a better life. Me? I never made it past Primary 3 before Ma made me hawk papers. Nothing should be so bad as to make a girl jump. You can always repeat an exam.

Pleased to finally connect with another being, Jonnie replied that this one couldn't have been doing too badly in school. After all, she was smart enough to figure out how to get to the top of Central Plaza, where roof access was probably prohibited... but his voice trailed off when the vendor woman ignored him, or didn't appear to hear him. In any case, she turned away and did not look at him again after their brief transaction. Now what, he wondered. It was time for breakfast and he was startled to find he was hungry. Surely, with all these *dai pai dongs* around him he could find a bowl of congee? Maybe even a stick of fried dough to go with it? He wandered east along Des Voeux towards the fragrant cooking smells of the wet market ahead until he found a food stall for congee. What year was this? Probably sometime in the 1950s or '60s, before he was born, since this stall had never existed in all the years he and Ma lived in Wan Chai. A sudden *eureka* moment: did death confine you to where you lived? If so, it could be worse than being stuck in Wan Chai for eternity, if this beginning of the rest of his death was anything to go by. His only regret was that he would miss out on his trip to Thailand, the one his girlfriend Wini booked.

On Monday night, he and Wini had found an inexpensive package tour to Phuket. She was so excited. He liked the way laugh lines crinkled her eyes when she smiled. Not that he would say this anymore, having once made the terrible mistake of doing so after he kissed her eyelids, because she immediately went into a panic about aging skin which he dismissed since she wasn't even thirty, too young to worry about all that. No, he said, just lines of laughter, they're beautiful. But she wouldn't listen. *What would men know about this*, she demanded. Every morning and night, she treated the skin around her eyes with some kind of collagen lotion, outrageously expensive. Which also meant he could only kiss her eyelids between the time she cleaned her face in the morning before she put on her makeup, or just after she removed her makeup at night and before she dabbed translucent gel from that tiny, overpriced tube. He regretted ever mentioning those lines, but that was him, always one foot in mouth when all he wanted was to speak his heart.

And now, no more now.

After breakfast, he went home. He didn't know where else to go. The building was there, as it had been long before his birth, and even before Ma moved in, pregnant with him out of wedlock when she was only twenty-two. Inside their flat, his mother was crying, and it broke his heart to hear that. Wini was with her. What time was it, when was this happening, but as he stood outside the door to the flat, he understood he no longer could judge time or space. The door of the neighbor's flat was different: it might have been a door from ten or fifty years earlier; when, he couldn't say. Their *tong lau* was pre the Second World War, so it held the possibility of elongated time. All he wanted was to go inside, to hold Wini in his arms and kiss her eyelids, to tell Ma he was sorry, it was not her fault, really, none of this was her fault. Was death an eternity of regret? The idea was too horrible to contemplate.

How to go inside? He didn't know and this confounded him. He pulled his key out of his pocket but it was a ghost key, usable only in ghost space. Logically, he knew this was after his death, but when? Did death take him into the future as well as the past, or was the future a linear unfolding? Jonnie wished he had paid more attention in school, asked more questions the way the thinking boys did, because perhaps it might have trained his mind better to figure out death. Like King-wah. He had gone to university and become a doctor. Sometimes, he wondered why King-wah was still their friend, him and the gang, since the rest of them had never gone past secondary, although Yuk-sing did get as far as an associate's degree and had succeeded in joining the police force as an inspector.

你不是! That girl's voice, out of nowhere, made him jump. He looked around but the wraith-like presence was nowhere to be seen. Her voice trailed away—*nei bat si, nei bat si*—repeating *you are not, you are not.* Jonnie tried to shut out the sound and concentrated on the voices behind the door.

Inside, Ma was inconsolable. Wini was saying, *don't be so* wounded-hearted, *we must carry on somehow.* As expected, Ma was blaming herself. *I shouldn't have put so much pressure on him, shouldn't have gotten into that argument. He was probably not paying attention when he crossed the road because he was upset.* No, Jonnie wanted to shout, that wasn't it at all, tell her Wini, tell her, because he figured his girlfriend would have gotten the full story from Yuk-sing by now. Besides, she knew about that argument. To his surprise, she didn't say anything, and just continued with the soothing platitudes. Why wasn't Wini telling Ma what she really needed to hear? Why?

Footfall on the staircase and he was surprised to see King-wah and Yuk-sing at the door of his home. Wini answered when they rang the doorbell, let them in, and then shut the door in his face. Jonnie stretched his hand tentatively towards the door, hoping it would go through. It didn't. Death was annoying, even more so than life. At least when you were alive, you understood how you existed. Would knowledge accumulate through experience the longer he was dead, or did death have different rules of engagement?

All this thinking made his head hurt, the way it did when Ma, or Wini, insisted on talking, talking, talking. Of course, women talked, he accepted that, and thought a lot (too much, as he often told King-wah, who, being a go-along-get-along guy, agreed, although Yuk-sing, who always disagreed with everything, would repeat *ad nauseam* that women held up half the sky so to quit being close-minded). Time passed, or at least he assumed it did, because the next thing he knew his two friends were leaving his home and he noticed a strange look pass between Yuk-sing and Wini, a look he couldn't fathom. Okay, so the thing to do was to follow them down the stairs into the streets and hover. It was the best connection he could make, and maybe, somehow, his voice or presence could make itself felt.

King-wah directed the pair to Pacific Coffee on Lockhart. Damn King-wah, always with the fancy coffees when a *cha chaan teng* should suffice. The trouble with education was that it turned people into snobs. The gang all came from this neighborhood, went through school together, and none of them were snobs, but university transformed King-wah into one. He lived in some fancy flat with his wife and kids in Pokfulam now, far away from the rest of them, and drove a

Merc. Even Yuk-sing wasn't the same guy, although he wasn't quite as bad. Besides, Lockhart was way on the other side, so why walk so far when there were plenty of *tea-food-restaurants* closer by? Jonnie realized his feet hurt from so much wandering around. Well, this sucked. Shouldn't death relieve you of bodily sensations, including fatigue? What kind of stupid universe was this? Would he also need to pee and shit? If so, where was he supposed to do that?

Over coffee, King-wah remarked that although the coroner's report said "accident due to hit-and-run," he couldn't help wondering if Chun-ying... Jonnie... had, as usual, not been paying attention?

"Probably," Yuk-sing responded.

"You know the way he is. Was."

"Yeah."

Hang on, Jonnie protested, as he hopped around their seats, surely the cops figured out that Bimmer ran the red, didn't they? Didn't modern technology record pretty much everything? Like on *CSI*? Couldn't you work out time of death down to the second and reconstruct the crime scene? It *was* a crime, after all.

King-wah said, "Who d'you suppose hit him?"

"I guess we'll never know."

It was the Bimmer, Jonnie shouted, that goddamned Bimmer! Find that bastard and drag him to court.

"The time of death was so early, 3:10 in the morning. Why was it reported so much later, what, like after four?"

Yuk-sing paused before replying, and Jonnie saw that strange look again, like the one that passed between him and

Wini. "My buddy in Accident Investigations said it was probably when his body fell off the canopy that someone finally noticed. From what they could tell, some speeder must have hit him, and somehow, he got flung up into that window and well, you know what happened with the glass." He stopped, sipped his cappuccino. "Poor bastard. Gruesome."

King-wah nodded. "Go on."

"What they figured was that he got stuck up there on the canopy, maybe partly lodged in the window frame, before he came unstuck and rolled onto the pavement."

"Dreadful."

"Yeah."

Shit! Shit! Shit! Shit! Jonnie's mind reeled. His death was blowing up out of all proportions. They didn't even get what happened right, never mind the time of death. He hadn't rolled off the canopy, he never was on it! What he recalled of that Tuesday morning of August 20, 2013, was that he had been hit, flung into the salon window and died at 5:55 a.m. Even his watch said so, the last thing he saw in the living world. How was it possible the police report could be so far off? Most of all, where was the gang that morning? Wouldn't they have been at Southorn? Wouldn't they all have seen the scene of the crime?

His friends had been speaking through his diatribe and were now standing, ready to leave. That was when he noticed they were both in dark suits.

"Ready?" King-wah said.

"As we'll ever be, I suppose."

"I wish Mrs. Tang and Wini would have come with us."

"Aaah, they probably wanted to be alone one last time."

Something like time shifted. Jonnie found himself at the North Point funeral home in a wake room. He was the deceased. How did he get here? Had he crossed the boundary of his neighborhood district to rejoin his body? Was that how it worked? Also, why couldn't he remember how he got here, or did memory operate by different rules in this un-alive state?

The last time he had attended a wake was a little over a year ago when their former math teacher, Mr. Chung, keeled over one morning in class and expired from a heart attack. The poor bastard was only fifty or so and he'd been one of the good *Ah-Sir's*, one who didn't drone on and on, who actually inspired his students. In fact, the only reason Jonnie managed to pass math in his School Cert exam was because Mr. Chung made him want to pay attention in class. The room had been overflowing with current students as well as former boys, many even older than his gang. If only Chung-Sir could have seen that! How proud he would have been.

And now here Jonnie was, paying respects at his own wake.

A closed casket sat beneath the large black and white photograph of him on the altar. His corpse must have been impossible to fix up. Maybe now, he could finally stop wandering around in this monstrous existence. Honestly, who knew death could be such a pain in the neck, literally and otherwise?

你不是! That girl's voice again. Was she following him? It turned into a sing-song taunt: *nei bat si, nei bat si, nei bat si* gradually morphing into 你是屍 *nei si si, nei si si!*

With a start, he saw that his wake was populated with the dead. Who were these people? Why had they come? He looked around to see if Chung was there, since that was one of the few dead people he did know, but the man was nowhere in sight. Neither was that girl. Only her voice was present, and it got louder and louder, her singsong punctuated with laughter. 你是屍! 你是屍! She had some nerve! *Nei si si!* Singing about him being a corpse as if it was a joke. Who the hell did she think she was? Meanwhile, the rest of the dead milled around in between the living. How odd. He instinctively knew which ones were dead and which living—not so hard since he recognized all the living people—but why did he know with such certainty that these others were dead? They all looked alive enough, just as the newspaper vendor and *dai pai dong* owner who served him the congee had looked alive. In fact, now that he thought about it, all those people earlier wandering around Wan Chai could have been alive, except somehow, he knew they were dead. The only exception had been that girl, the suicide who *looked* dead because she was all banged up from her jump.

He panicked. Had he been wandering around all this time in a state of partial decapitation? If so, how *awful.* He rushed forward to the coffin to peer at the small mirror on the altar, but it was too high and even though he tried jumping up, he couldn't see himself. The coffin! He climbed on it, but the curved lid made him lose his balance and he landed with a thud on the ground. This was ridiculous. His own coffin wouldn't even give him a leg up. What kind of wake was this?

Such inconvenience was no way to honor him. And now, his butt hurt.

He moved towards the glass walls of the room. The quick and the dead were reflected there, but try as he might, he could not see himself. Okay, was this because he was only half dead (perhaps the suicide girl was as well)? Or maybe his head was detached and hanging too far down to be reflected? The more he tried to work out what was happening, the more frustrated he became. Jonnie hated thinking long about anything, preferring instead to make quick decisions and move on. The joy of living was, for him, getting off work, going dancing, shooting hoops with his buddies, and eating. And making love to Wini. She was sweet and immensely pliable in bed. What more should a guy need?

His gang arrived. Hey, he said, here I am. Useless, because his spectral self was clearly not affecting anyone. His mother was seated in the front row, weeping, Wini by her side. That was it for intimates, he thought with a pang. All he had were his friends and Wini. He glanced at the dead, shuffling around his coffin, commenting on his photo and the funeral arrangements, making fun of the small number of mourners. Don't be so mean, he wanted to say, not all of us have big families or lots of friends! My mother worked hard her whole life. She didn't have time to socialize.

What he did say was *shut the fuck up!* The sing-song voice of that girl continued to follow him around. It was softer now, but Jonnie heard it continuously, rising and falling in volume, like a mosquito swooping around his ear.

A familiar voice was speaking behind him and he turned,

surprised to see his supervisor from work. What was that loser doing here? The man bowed to the coffin and then took a seat next to some of his other colleagues. Perhaps he was making up for the bad annual review he had given Jonnie last week, saying he needed to be more punctual. Hell, he'd only be late a few times. Their records were wrong because there was absolutely no way he could have been late as many times as they said. Jonnie worked at the airport in aircraft maintenance, and had done so since he left school and had been accepted into their training program. Ma had been so proud. *My son works for HAECO*, she bragged to everyone. Large company, good prospects, stable job. But what Ma hoped was for him to become an aircraft engineer, but that required a higher diploma. Even Wini agreed. *You have the basic requirements in physics and math*, she said. *How hard would it be? Plus the pay's better.* It was all he could do to stay in the job, although he'd never tell them that. Jonnie hated shift work, because the irregular schedule interfered with his dancing. If he had his way he'd work in a nightclub, serving drinks perhaps, but the one time he mentioned that casually to Wini, she said *how cheap, how shameful* and wouldn't speak to him for days. So that ended that. Well, definitely too late now.

Then the wake ended and everyone was at the crematorium. An incendiary blast and it was all over. He was back in Wan Chai. What the fuck? Didn't he at least get to join the dinner? Man, what a lousy deal. What else did death cheat you of? This was really worse than being alive, and that had been bad enough.

That girl's voice echoed, a smile in her whisper. *You are*

not! You are corpse!

A conversation of the living from around the street corner entered his auditory range. Jonnie strained to hear.

"She'll be okay."

"I feel so terrible for her, but what else can I do?"

Wasn't that Wini's voice? He tried to see who she was talking to but found he couldn't move to where the voices came from.

"You've done enough, more than enough under the circumstances. Come on, let me take you home."

"Sure."

"But not just yet, okay?"

"Please Yuk-sing, not right now."

"I'm sorry, I know this is bad, but I can't help it."

Wait, what was going on with Yuk-sing? What did he mean? He was near the Police Headquarters on Arsenal, somewhere along Harcourt. The voices were coming from further away. No matter how hard he tried, he was up against an invisible barrier that he couldn't go through. It was just like that TV series on the English channel Ma liked to watch, where a town was imprisoned under an invisible dome. He had been surprised when she started watching it because she never watched English TV. When he asked her why all of a sudden, she only said, *why not? There are Chinese subtitles.*

It was dark. Annoyed that his dead eyes were not able to see any better than his alive ones through the evening light, he cast his gaze into the distance, willing himself to see Wini, because by now, he was certain it was her voice and Yuk-sing's. Their voices got louder and he heard his friend say, *you know how I feel, how we feel about each other. It would only have been a matter of time.* And then he heard Wini sob as if her heart would break. Yuk-sing's car came into view and he parked in the police compound. Jonnie found himself right next to the car and inside, Wini and Yuk-sing were kissing each other, a long, passionate kiss of lovers, and then, everything made sense.

No! You can't! His voiceless shout floated into dead silence. No, he said, what did I ever do to you, to either of you, that you should betray me like this? They were both dressed as they had been earlier at the wake—even in that somber dress, Wini had been so sexy he had gotten hard, unsure how pleased he felt at the continuance of that bodily function—so this was the same evening. The same evening!

Yuk-sing was caressing her, his hands all over her body. Jonnie stared at them, unable to avert his gaze. She was letting him touch her between her legs, even pulling his hand closer to her crotch. How could this be?

A voice from behind startled him.

It's like an algebraic equation, the voice said. If A equals B and B equals C, then A must equal C, yet all you ever wanted to know was *but what do you mean by A?*

Jonnie turned around and saw Chung, his former math teacher. Ah sir! What are you doing here?

I'm trying to explain B. Don't you remember? You wouldn't listen for so long, insisting that A didn't make sense and therefore nothing made sense. You're A and Wini is B. Yuk-sing is C. He always was late to life, even in school, but better late than never, right, right? Chung was chuckling. The familiar voice, reassuring, gently prodding, calmed Jonnie.

Chung sir, why am I here?

Why do you think?

Er, because I'm dead?

Something like that.

But why does that girl's voice keep following me around?

Why? Come on, think!

You know me, I hate to think.

Then you'll never know, will you?

With that Mr. Chung drifted away.

Jonnie was about to race after him but couldn't. Wini and Yuk-sing were going at it. Her skirt was hiked up so far her panties were visible, as was his hand sliding under the thin fabric, yanking it off with her help. He was disgusted, appalled, but couldn't look away. She was letting him unbutton her blouse with his other hand, which was sliding under her bra. He couldn't look away.

Wini was a manicurist at Princess Nail. She got the job after graduating from beauty college and had been working in the Causeway Bay salon for a couple of years when she and Jonnie met. It had taken Jonnie ten months of persuasion before she would go to a love motel with him, and even then, she wouldn't go all the way. They were more or less engaged before she finally surrendered over two years later, and even though he tried to be gentle, he knew it hurt her, and this was a memory he disliked.

Yet here she was, now, virtually fucking Yuk-sing in his car.

He could see the bulge of his friend's crotch. Wini was unbuckling his belt, unzipping him, and he watched, horrified as she pulled out his penis and bent down to suck it. The first time Jonnie suggested they do that, she'd made a face and called him disgusting. No matter how sweetly he tried, her answer was always no, absolutely not, and that was that. Yet here she was, doing it, and clearly, it wasn't her first time. Jonnie was ashamed for her. It was like watching a porn flick except that the last thing he wanted to do was jerk off.

Voices from around the corner, and suddenly, Wini and Yuk Sing were scrambling, rearranging their disheveled clothes. She slid down low into the seat, but what startled him was how much she was giggling, instead of being embarrassed. Where was the Wini he knew, the oh-so-proper girl who slapped his hand if it strayed too close to her ass or boobs in public? Not even in public, just when they were with their friends? What had happened to his beautiful, good girl, who was sexy in private for him and him alone? Who was this stranger he was so sure loved him, who was so kind to Ma, who was there for him in the mornings even when he had been bad, out too late drinking and dancing the night before, without her?

The more he thought, the more his head hurt and the more irritated he became.

I'm here, he said to no one.

Hey Ma, he shouted, being dead is overrated so stop saying you might as well be dead, which was her favorite thing to say. Which was what started their argument that afternoon, in just a kidding way at first until Ma said, *well what is there to live for if all you'll ever be is just a low-paid worker, if you won't better yourself,* and then he'd yelled at her, said all she cared about was money and walked out, slamming the door. He went home to Wini, hoping for solace and sex. She told him to calm down, his mother wouldn't stay mad but then dismissed him, saying she had to get ready for work. That night he called work to say he was sick and went dancing instead. Alone.

Wan Chai was hemming him in.

He turned away from Yuk-sing's car, invisible to Wini who was still giggling, saying *I can't find my panties.*

A breeze whisked past him as that voice whispered-sang *you are not, you are corpse.*

Something like time passed and the next thing he knew there were Yuk-sing and Wini, at the Pacific Coffee with King-wah, and they were telling him about them. How they couldn't help it. How terrible they felt. How they didn't know what to do next but what they really wanted to do was get married because, it turned out, Wini was pregnant. *Wait,* he shouted, *what if it's my baby,* but as usual, no one heard him. He wasn't sure how much time had elapsed so possibly, just possibly, it could be Yuk-sing's but somehow Jonnie didn't quite believe that. Why didn't he know? Surely death should give him more access to information like that? Was he doomed to wonder forever? Could he not, telepathically, know the DNA of the unborn child?

Silence. Nothing, not even the sound of the song that pursued him.

This world of the living was driving him crazy. He had to

get away from all their deceptions and lies and petty carping. Jonnie wandered out of the Pacific Coffee and headed back to Southorn Playground. And there she was, that suicide girl, all scrunched and scarred, her school uniform so short it was some kind of sexy come-on. He wondered if she would shout-sing at him again, but she seemed a lot calmer now, less tragic. She stretched out her hand and asked, *want to come along?* He glared at her, angry at this whole mess of his death and life. Where, where did she expect him to go? *Home, of course,* she replied and he realized they were communicating now, even though he couldn't make sounds and couldn't really hear her, not the way you could in the living world. *Haven't you had enough,* said a voice, from somewhere beyond the suicide girl. *Never mind about B and C, you're A,* the voice continued. Chung-sir! Jonnie shouted, I can't figure it out. *Don't try so hard just hear what she's telling you.* Wini, Yuk-sing, his baby, or was it? It would be their baby, regardless. *Want to come along,* the girl asked again. He looked at her, scrunched, sexy, dead, as she taunted him, saying, *come on, follow me or I'll start sing-ing again. Nei bat si, nei si...* No! he shouted. Stop! I'll go, I'll go. And that was the moment everything began to make sense at last.

KASPAR'S WARP

for Al Montanaro, in memoriam

S URPRISINGLY, **the bathroom door is ajar.** *Gu Kwun pushes it, gingerly, so that it swings open a little but not completely. The back of his mother's head is just above the tub, and he wonders at her bathing with the door unlocked. What worries him more is the thought of seeing her naked. He is nine.*

When she does not respond to—are you having breakfast? —*he prods the door further open and steps halfway in. The water looks cold. No steam fills the room, the mirror is clear. His mother's eyes are closed. Gu Kwun averts his eyes from her nakedness and touches her arm. No life.*

In the kitchen he opens the freezer. Where has all this ice come from? Stacks of trays, more than he can ever recall. Emptying the cubes into a bucket, he thinks about making more ice. In the bathroom, he drains the water, piles the ice over his mother's body. Then, he leaves. Closes the door.

Six days pass. Home is as it always has been. His books sit neatly on the desk in his bedroom. On the seventh morning, he gets dressed for school and sits at the dining table waiting for breakfast. But Conchita does not appear, smiling jo sun, *carrying two white bowls of steaming congee on a tray. Their live-in Filipino domestic*

*helper has vanished the way his mother has. He glances at the shut
bathroom door. He hasn't used the bathroom for almost a week.*

*At school during break, Gu Kwun looks for Space Gang—Caspar, Janie, Kazuo and Shalini—but they're not in their usual corner. In fact, the school is filled with faces he doesn't recognize. Even
the teachers seem different. How many more days will he wander
around like this, waiting for his friends to return, for Conchita to
walk out of the kitchen smiling, for his mother to wake up?*

Caspar Mak quit Word, abandoning his fiction once again.
Hopeless. He never got beyond this point in trying to write
about his dead childhood friend. "Kaspar's Warp"—where the
dead went about their daily lives, their consciousness tethered
to the structure of their worlds, unable to desist despite the
truth—well, it was a stupid idea, a poor imitation of every
paranormal tale ever written. All he knew was somehow, that
Warp needed to petrify to resurrect the dead. Like Anderson's
Tin Soldier. Was death tin? And what about the paper ballerina? Give it up. He would never be a writer, despite what his
friends and teachers believed.

Fatigued, he surfed the news.

Caspar was sixteen and what he most wanted was to move
back home. He'd returned yesterday. Why he had to go to a
prep school in Massachusetts, while his parents continued to
live and work in Hong Kong, was beyond him. *Time's* Person
of the Year is YOU, he read, meaning the web and its worldwide connectivity. Dumb. Equating people with technology
was like the one-legged soldier's love for a dancer because he
thought she was also, like him, one-legged, when really, her

petrified state was just the arabesque. It was what you didn't see that got you. Like Gu Kwun, his best friend. Bitten by a snake and dead at the age of seven. Ten years later, he was still in perpetual mourning, or something perilously close.

His cell phone buzzed, break-danced on the desk top. Unfamiliar number. He tapped the speaker icon. "Yea?"

The familiar voice, airy, shy, just a hint of mischief, "Space bunny?"

His heart twirled. "Janie Hammond. You're really back."

"Little late, better than never. Kaz and Shalini said you'd be home for the holidays."

Strawberry blond wisps blowing across her face, an impatient hand brushing them away. Janie. His crush and valentine at six, nine, twelve, until, at fourteen, he saw Jimmy Wong kiss her and he pouted a year, stopped talking to her, and then she was gone, her dad transferred back to *The Wall Street Journal* in New York. Kaz and Shalini said *serves you right, dork!* He masturbated to her memory for two years and then was sent to the States, just as her dad was transferred back to Hong Kong. Life wasn't just unfair, it was insane.

Janie and Gu Kwun and Caspar. Space Gang. From kindergarten, they migrated together into grade school at HKIS where Shalini and Kaz joined them. Only Janie would dare use that silly nickname now. Even Shalini, despite her outrageousness, wouldn't dream of it. Caspar and Shalini were the two who weren't at least partially American, no longer unusual at American International. His parents were Canto Hong Kong workaholics, Harvard B-School. Which made him a noisy, not quiet American-to-be. But Space Gang wasn't about the right passports, residences, or degrees. Their families had too many to keep straight, and were entirely too loud about how things had to be.

They missed their quiet one, Chak Gu Kwun.

Christmas Eve. The city aglow with too much neon, tinsel, gigantic Hello Kitty look-alikes as the four of them circled the levels of Pacific Place mall, trying to forget their futures. Caspar was trying even harder to keep his hands off Janie who had become—and this he still didn't quite believe—willowy *and* edgy, irresistible.

"Hate it," she said, in response to his query about school in New York. "Detest, despise, deplore it. Like every bad high school movie. Don't miss it at all."

"So tell us," Shalini said, "how's New York?"

Kaz laughed, hugged his now-girlfriend. The two became an item last term after Caspar left. Shalini almost half a head taller, in heels. It upset Caspar's sense of symmetry, but Kaz looked constantly content now where he'd always been a wreck, the worst pill popper, so this probably was a good thing?

Janie was pointing at a revolving doll four levels down that looked like "a mutant crossed between a dog and a chicken." In a red and green tutu, it stood high against some gigantic logo. Tchaikovsky's "Sugar Plum Fairy" was tinkling, loud enough to deafen the atrium. "Could Christmas get any more demented? It's even worse than I remembered."

Caspar lightly punched her. "Oh so maybe New York's not so bad?"

"It's not New York, or America. Just high school there. College will be different, that's what Dad says."

"You sure about that?"

"Positive."

The group assented. Mr. Hammond was the only truly cool parent they had.

The four stopped at the top level of the mall, slouched against the barrier, each facing a different direction, murmured groupspeak. Comfortable. Sane. Caspar felt he had never been away, that it hadn't been almost two and a half years since he'd last seen Janie, that Gu Kwun was still with them.

Kaz spoke first: "So what would GK study?"

"Economics," Caspar said. "Then the MBA at Harvard like his mom."

Shalini smiled. "Law. Just to be different. And then he'd defend every Chinese dissident who ended up in jail."

"Medicine," Kaz offered. "Like his father. That way Dr. Chak would finally pay attention to him."

Janie looked away. The others waited. Casper thought she looked sad, but then, they were all sad, remembering GK, his fierce mother, his patience, his striking stubbornness when he knew he was right.

She said, "He'd go to art school."

They went silent. She was right. GK was real talent, and when they played at Janie's, her father remarked upon that. *I will be an artist*, he declared, a month before he died. *Your mother?* Caspar asked, but GK brushed it aside, *she'll want what's best for me. If I tell her that's what's best, she'll trust me.*

Caspar pictured GK's tall mother, a serious-faced investment banker whom they all were afraid of although they never told him that. GK saying, politely, that he was going to art school. She, furious. Livid. GK insisting, never raising his voice. The imagined scene made Caspar happy.

Shalini, finally: "Ten years ago. Thanksgiving. Remember the funeral? His grandmother never stopped crying."

Kaz squeezed her hands, brought them to his lips.

Janie straightened up, raised her bottled water. "To GK."

The others echoed: "To GK."

Afterward, when Caspar and Janie were alone, he worked up the nerve to take her hand. She didn't resist. It was like that with them, this lack of resistance, just as he wished he could take the path of least resistance, to maybe study philosophy, write fiction, and eventually try for the MFA, Iowa or Michigan, which he could present to his parents as the Ivies of writing. His teachers were telling him do it, that his talent shouldn't be wasted. He told Janie all this. Why had he ever allowed his wrath to come between them? He told her about "Kaspar's Warp," the story where he simply couldn't see the ending. When they parted, she kissed him high up on his cheek, grazing his ear. "Send me your story when it's done. I'd love to read it."

Afterward, he heard her voice again, the night Jimmy Wong ambushed her with that publicly passionate kiss, his hands sliding down her butt as they danced—*I didn't want him to. It wasn't supposed to*—and shuddered at his horrifying jealousy, his unreasonable rage as he shouted across the party room, *slut, slut, fucking bitch!*

Janie and Gu Kwun. *And me.* That was how it had been, him as the extra. Even though they were far too young then for that to have mattered, it mattered to him, always had. It was what was wrong with him, what made him different from the others who could do what they were supposed to in life.

Afterward, he took the long way home, knowing it wouldn't matter on Christmas Eve because both his parents would be working, doing whatever they did behind closed doors up to the last hour, minute, second of their days. Sundays or holidays didn't make any difference. Each kept an office at home.

The MTR was packed and Caspar had to wait through two trains. He considered walking—it wasn't that far from Admiralty to Causeway Bay to catch the minibus up Braemar Hill—but his mother would undoubtedly ask him how he got back, he couldn't lie to her, and then she'd go on and on about how it wasn't a good idea to walk in Hong Kong, especially along Queen's Road East where the pavement often narrowed, because drivers were so careless. As if she knew. His mother never walked except in shopping malls. What she wanted was for him to take a taxi, but Caspar didn't want to be like everyone else, taking taxis everywhere, acting like they owned the world (never mind that at least here in their bubble of a city, they did). Because they were, as Shalini declared, "the privileged offspring of those who more or less run the world," and their futures, or so they had been told since forever, was to live to own that world.

The train jerked to a stop and he spilled out with the crowds, trying to stay his course. They all had their courses ahead. Shalini a doctor who must refuse the arranged marriage. She'd dated Chinese, French, and now Kaz, Japanese-Brazilian from New Jersey. No defaulting to some ancient Indian despite her grandparents in Delhi. Kaz was just Kaz, geek, nerd, computer fanatic who once hacked into the Hong Kong government's website, only to declare it too lame to bother with further. Some kind of genius. Janie would be the journalist, or researcher who worked for NGOs. Her father had custody since the parents' divorce, so she could mostly ignore the carping of her Canto-freakish, over-achieving mom. Okay for girls to over-achieve and do the career since some decent guy would come along, especially for someone as intelligent, kind, and drop-dead gorgeous as her. But boys, they had to succeed in the right life, marry the Chinese wife. At least, boys like him did. His parents didn't even know about Space Gang. His mother *definitely* didn't know about Janie. Yet Space Gang—even now he embraced that childish name—was where he came alive.

The minibus took off and chugged uphill, rounded the bend. His building came into view. Disembarked. Rode the lift up. Passing fourteen, his throat caught. Like yesterday that they were both seven, Gu Kwun saying, *this is me*, and he, *okay, see ya*. The lift door opened at twenty-two. He stood at his door. Both his parents' shoes were neatly lined up outside. He positioned his key. Waited.

Gu Kwun stands outside the bathroom and places his ear against the door, trying to hear the sound of water. His mother is taking a bath. That must be it. What other explanation is there? His mother is taking a bath. In a little while, his mother will emerge wearing her bathrobe. She'll go into her room, close the door, get dressed. Then, Conchita will serve dinner and the two of them will eat together and he'll tell her all about his day at school. That's what has to happen because nothing else is acceptable.

What couldn't he see?

Time sped up. University split them: Shalini and Kaz off to the UK; Janie, Stanford; he, Harvard, where he took a little philosophy and even creative writing. Electives. His mother didn't care as long as he majored in economics and his GPA didn't slide below 3.85, which it never did. Graduation, Janie's text: *so, MFA?* He hesitated, texted back: *Law.* Her reply: *WTF?!* He did not respond.

Time sputters. Petrifies. The present arrives and he is a second-year law student.

One day in the library, fatigued by too many words on the page, he is surprised by her text from Hong Kong. *Hey u ok?* No, he wants to say, no, I am most assuredly not okay. But that is not an acceptable response.

He scrolls through his notes, hits save but goes to the wrong folder, the one marked FICTION, unopened for a long while. "Kaspar's Warp" sits there, untouched. He recalls her wish to read it. He meant to send it. No reason now, he doesn't think, and files his notes on contract law into the folder where the rest of his life resides.

ALL ABOUT SKIN

for my muse Jenny Wai

I WENT **to Derma the week before Christmas to buy an** *american* **skin.** I was apprehensive because Derma's expensive and doesn't allow trade-ins. But their salesman gave me credit on pretty generous terms, and let me take it away the same day, which made me feel good.

This was not an impulse purchase, you understand. I've been pricing *americans* for donkeys' years. My last topskin, which I got fourteen years ago at Epiderm International, was an *immigranta*. It was okay, but only really fit if teamed with the right accessories. That got to be a pain. Going *american*, though, is a big step. After Derma, there's no place else to go but down, at least as long as they're number one.

You see, my history with skins is spotty. I stay with one a long time, sometimes too long, because change makes me itch. The thing about an old skin is that even if it's worn or stained, it hangs comfortably because you know where it needs a bit of a stretch or a quick fold and tuck. Before *immagranta*, I wore *cosmopol* for seven years. The latter was always a wee bit shiny between the legs, although I knew enough to deflect glare with *corpus ceiling-glass*, my preferred underskin, from

SubCutis.

But I'm getting ahead of myself. A chronology of my history with skins will keep names and dates straight. It's sort of like skinning a lion. First, you have to shoot the beast.

Like most folks on our globe, I got my first topskin from my parents on my eighth birthday. Now I know there are some who start off at six or even as young as five, like the wearers of *nipponicas* and *americans*. We were a conservative family, though, and when I slipped into *china cutis*, the only product line People's PiFu sold back then, I was the proudest little creature strutting around Hong Kong. This was in the 1960s. My idea of skin began and ended with *china cutis*, basic model.

Mind you, there's nothing wrong with basics. This one gave me room to breathe and plenty of growing space. During the teenage-diet thing, it adapted nicely enough, although Ma worried about premature tummy sags. You know what mothers are like. If there isn't a real problem to worry about, they'll find one.

For years, I simply didn't think about skin. Passing exams was all that mattered so that I too could be a face-valued citizen. I practiced tending to wounds and cuts, bruises and scars, sores and boils. What fascinated me were bites—a plethora of bug nibbles bursting out on the back of my thighs; fang prints snakes sank into my ankles; crab kisses slashing my fingers; teeth marks dogs lodged in my shoulder. Papa was pallid the day I came home from the beach, my back and arms covered with huge red splotches. They looked awful but didn't itch, which was merciful, and disappeared the next day. Sand crabs,

Ma said. Durable, my old *china cutis*. There are days I miss it.

My problem began round about age nineteen. Being ambitious types, my parents packed me off to schools abroad. I salivated at Derma's store windows in New York, desperate for an *american*. They were all the rage, and outrageously expensive. "You can buy that yourself when you're earning your own money," Papa declared. "I can't afford it." I stormed and pouted, scratching my face and legs till they bled, giving Ma something to really cry about. He wouldn't relent. It wasn't just the money. He and Ma had worn their *china cutises* since they were eight and couldn't see why I wouldn't do likewise. From their perspective, I was acting like a spoiled brat. They were right, I suppose, but you find me a nineteen-year-old who isn't stuffed full of the fashion of her times.

So I passed the exams, got my face-valued citizen parchment, and by my mid-twenties had this great job in advertising. Paris three times a year! Imagine. It was a pretty exciting life, I must say, despite my skin.

In the spring of '79, I dared to visit Integume of Paris.

If you think Derma's hot, you've never shopped at Integume. From the moment you enter their store—no, store's too pedestrian—their boutique, you're engulfed by the unimaginable possibilities of skin. Moisturizer wafts through the atmosphere. Never, never, it whispers, will even the tiniest blemish dare to mar this surface. *Jamais!* You wander around this cutaneous paradise where an array of products tempts you with seductive promise: *euro trash tannis, decadence glorious, romance du monde ancien, french chic...* skins! Meters upon meters of skins, both natural and quality synthetic, draped fetchingly, lovingly, placed with the kind of care that plunges skin-deep.

The saleslady offered to take my old *china cutis* in trade, saying it was in big demand and commanded good resale value. Secondhands were rare because few wearers upgraded abroad back then. I really didn't care one way or another because I was sick to death of *china cutis*. I mean, it couldn't tan or wrinkle, and even a little makeup made me feel all Suzie Wong. The only reason I stuck it out so long was, well, family is family after all. But enough is enough. It was time to go *cosmopol.*

The beauty of *cosmopol* is its flexibility. I could slip in and out of it into something more comfortable whenever I wanted-ed. *China cutis* stuck to me like a fragile layer of dried rice glue. It flaked periodically—showers of scarf skin—and had to be treated with such respect. That was the worst part, the respect. Four thousand years of R&D had gone into its design. Personally, I thought the design had already run its course, but then, I've always been "one step too many beyond," as Ma says. When Mao, the primo *china cutis* wearer of the last century created a big to-do by jumping into the Yellow River, thus proving its durability, it was downright asinine.

But the truth of the matter is my *china cutis* had gotten loose and sloppy. Fashion-wise, the look was making a come-back by then, but not in any real way. Mine sagged. I wallowed in free space. Ma had suggested I return it for a newer model, but those weren't a marked improvement. People's PiFu hadn't modernized their product line for global consumption yet. It was just an ill-destined style.

So I traded it in. My father would've killed me had he known. He didn't, though, thanks to *cosmopol.*

I owe a lot to that Integume saleslady. She showed me how to enhance my *cosmopol* skin with separates and coordinates. Stuck with *china cutis*, I didn't know about all the accessory lines. I confess I was pretty extravagant for a while there. From Integume, I went to SubCutis where I bought three underskins—a *sub-four seas, lady don juan* and *corporate rung.* They were expensive, but worth it. Like the saleslady said, you make the big one-time investment and add extras as you go. Besides, Integume allowed layaway, and SubCutis was running a special promotion for customers of Integume. A year later, I added *underwired g-strung* and *corpus-ceiling glass* to my skinrobe. All in all, I made out okay.

Being able to slip any one of these over or under *cosmopol* was such a liberation. If I were feeling particularly daring, I could combine accessories by themselves. None of them worked that well solo, probably because they were all synthetic. *Underwired g-strung* slid off at the slightest provocation. *Corporate rung* was generally a tight fit, although the crotch was absurdly loose. The designer hadn't quite gotten the hang of that one, especially in female petite.

The real test, though, was passing muster with Papa. By wearing *cosmopol* with *sub-four seas* underneath, I could fool him into thinking I had on my *china cutis.* Things were looking good. But none of this explains why, after a good seven years, I decided to give up *cosmopol* for an *immigranta.*

To tell you properly, I have to go back to Derma and their *american* line. You have to understand that I never lost my yen for *american*. I'm a sucker for advertising, and Derma could really launch a marketing campaign. Even though they'd only been around a couple of centuries, everyone thought they were the real thing. It was a question of focus. Their entire strategy depended on narrowing everything down to one product. Derma equaled *american*. The same idea worked for People's PiFu a few centuries earlier. Their problem was different—times had changed and they hadn't. Renaming their company and sticking on a new logo back in the late 1940s was not sufficient to create the fundamental transformation they desperately needed.

But during the years I ran around in *cosmopol*, Derma had been steadily losing market share to All Nippon Cutis.

Let me digress a moment. All Nippon Cutis were smart. They invested in R&D for some ten years to produce a top quality *american*-like skin. I read about them in *Forbes*. Their chairman sent fifty of their top designers and executives to Paris for two years to check out Integume's styles. After that, those same folks went to New York for another two years to study Derma's market leadership. By the time they actually started designing in Tokyo, they had the marketplace all figured out.

The world, they decided, wanted Derma's strength with Integume's flair. Somehow, the frivolous fun inherent in Sub-Cutis needed to be integrated. The smartest thing All Nippon Cutis did was to compete in Derma's primary marketplace, which was an easier target than Integume's international market dominance.

You know the rest. At the beginning, the very rich would

fly to Tokyo to buy an *america dreama*. By the mid-eighties, All Nippon Cutis had opened branches all over the U.S. You remember their commercials—Lincoln's head superimposed on the Statue of Liberty crying "Cutify!" Market forces being what they are, within a year, you could get an *america dreama* out in Jersey for half the price of Derma's *american*.

Their *america dreama* impressed me. They couldn't call it *american*, of course, because of trademark infringement. I had moved to New York by then, but Ma told me that the product was a big hit even in Hong Kong. In Tokyo, it became very fashionable as a second skin to *nipponica*.

At that time, I wouldn't have dreamed of buying from Derma. Not only was my *cosmopol* still serviceable, but Derma's prices were quite unjustified. Oh I know they were all natural, while All Nippon Cutis used blends, but big deal, my old *china cutis* was all natural too. Even when the hoopla about *american dreama* turning yellow after repeated sun exposure made the news, no one cared, not really, because, first of all, the scientists who claimed that were working for Derma, and most people had begun to believe that skins should be replaced after even as little as three to five years. I find that a little wasteful myself, but All Nippon Cutis made a good point by offering to recycle old skins.

As impressive as it was, I wasn't quite sold on what amounted to only a make-believe *american*. Which meant my alternative was Epiderm International, makers of *immigranta*, *asia personals*, and *ec*, among others.

My problem was that *cosmopol* wasn't fitting quite right.

Life in New York was expensive enough without keeping

up my *cosmopol* skin. It was flexible, but only if pampered a lot. You needed the best face creams and lotions, and could only be seen in the most fashionable places. Worst of all, it radiated this worldly air, while hinting at a sexual undertow, but avoiding any engagements that would ravage its surface charms. Debt did not aid its sustenance, as I was still paying off my balance at Integume.

At least *cosmopol* could be cashed in. Unlike *china cutis*, which had great trade-in value but generated no cash, New Yorkers would kill for secondhand *cosmopols*. I actually made a profit, because naturally, with the original trade-in, I hadn't paid full price, although the interest alone was staggering.

For almost six months, I went around without a main skin. Luckily, I had all those secondary ones. Depending on my mood, I usually wore either *corporate rung* or *corpus-ceiling glass*, with *sub-four seas* underneath. It was an uncomfortable time. I was sometimes tempted to slip on *lady don juan* with *underwired g-strung* to get back that *cosmopol* feeling, but was just too embarrassed. I hated admitting I didn't have a main skin, but I needed to pay down debt, even if not completely, before my next investment.

The day I purchased my *immigranta*, I dreamt about flying back to Hong Kong to see my parents. This was the real reason to lose *cosmopol*. Lying to them was fine when I was younger, but now, it made me feel like a hypocrite. It wasn't their fault I didn't like *china cutis*. They couldn't have foreseen my life.

Even then, it was another six years before I finally made it home. I had retired *lady don juan* and *underwired g-strung* to my back closet, because the market for those secondary styles had pretty much gone bust. You remember the beginning of the dual skin craze. Anyone who was anyone wouldn't dream of being without a second skin. SubCutis hung on, but just barely. Word flew on the street that they were going to file Chapter 11. I won that bet when they succumbed to a buyout by All Nippon Cutis. You have to figure there's a niche market somewhere for their questionable lines. Besides, the rest of their products did have mainstream appeal.

It was a big bet, which was good, because the money paid for my trip home. I had left advertising and was working on the fringes of Wall Street, a bad place to be post Black Monday. With my debt on *immigranta*, I lived paycheck to paycheck. Maybe I was sticking my neck out unnecessarily with that bet. But the great thing about my *immigranta* skin was that it absorbed immunity to risk.

I suppose that's why I kept it so long. I didn't have to lie to my parents because it was the one other acceptable skin in their eyes. Call them old-fashioned, but they like the chameleon complexion of *immigranta*, especially because on me, it looked enough like *china cutis*. What they didn't know was that I had slipped *golden peril* on underneath. I'd picked that one up cheap at a SubCutis fire sale before going to see them. I'm awfully thankful for fickle fashion trends; products in a downturn sometimes prove extremely attractive, given the right circumstances.

So why *american* now? You might say I got caught up in the wave of market forces, because I'm past much of that fashion stuff. Derma went through some pretty shaky years, losing considerable market share to All Nippon Cutis, who took their range way out there with *ho-ho hollywoodo*. Tacky, I think, but who could predict its huge appeal, from Los Angeles to Beijing? Even Epiderm International horned in on Derma's territory with their Epiderm US subsidiary, whose *emigrantis* and *global villager* became ludicrously popular. All Nippon Cutis retaliated quickly enough with *worldo warrior*. For awhile there, I almost shed *immigranta* for one of these newer models.

Derma had it all wrong. Their feeble attempt to launch *heritage hides* was laughable. Imagine thinking Mr. Ed singing "Got to Know about History" would make any impact? I think it was voted the worst commercial of 1988. Price was another factor. Some say they priced themselves out of their own marketplace.

Derma refused to entertain the idea of growth even though revenues were down 30% and profits almost non-existent. In the meantime, All Nippon Cutis merged with the largest hairbank in Frankfurt, while Epiderm was borrowing heavily both in London and New York to finance their expansion. *The Wall Street Journal* suggested that Epiderm's reliance on junk bonds would be their undoing, but you couldn't be too critical of junk in those days. Even Integume dived right in, expanding and grabbing share in markets like Moscow, Shanghai, and Prague, as well as in places like Cincinnati, Seattle, and Minneapolis, where *cosmopol* became more popular than *american*. By now, Derma was a distant number four behind those three global leaders, at least in sales and profits. If you count market size, People's PiFu is right up there, but of course, prices aren't comparable, given their rock bottom manufacturing costs.

In the end, everything turned on principle, plus a little Chinese intrigue.

You've heard the conspiracy theories, about how the CIA negotiated with Soong & Dong to flood the global market with synthetic epidermatis. There are even whispers that it had to do with WTO membership for the motherland. I don't believe those rumors myself, but you must admit the sudden availability of top-quality synthetic raw material, at a third of the prevailing price per kilo, was unprecedented. Ever since the worldwide skin crisis of the seventies, the industry's been wary of shortages. Survival has depended on reducing costs, which meant going synthetic.

Price wars raged. Folks started buying five, ten, even as many as twenty topskins, never mind the multiples in underskins. Even my parents each bought a second, although Ma complained that synthetic just didn't feel as good. Suddenly, skin took on a whole new dimension. The markets for other bodyparts went into shock, unable to compete against this surge in demand for skin and only skin. Meanwhile, futures in natural epidermatis were priced 25% up even in the nearest months, which battered Derma. Rumor had it they were buying supplies from People's PiFu, who of course didn't suffer an iota, given their government-regulated market.

And then, in the middle of 1997, the worldwide skin market crashed.

It was bound to happen. Folks were carrying debt over their heads in skins. Even with cheaper prices, an average one still comprises a hefty percentage of most incomes. Besides, as Papa declared, how many skins can a person wear anyway? Used, recycled, and even slightly defective new skins flooded the stores. Now, everyone's fancy skins were worth less than a mound of toenails.

Things looked bleak.

Folks are funny. They self-correct pretty quickly in the face of disaster. Everyone laid low on skins for awhile. Television pundits compare the past few years to the Great Eyelash Famine as well as the New Deal in Teeth. I don't pay much attention to pundits myself. They invent connections where there are none.

Derma's comeback was quite the media circus. Among the larger companies, they had the upper hand now because they hadn't invested in growth, and consequently, weren't sitting on useless inventory or excessive debt. There's nothing quite like cash, is there? But I have to admire their new CEO for some pretty quick moves. First, there was the hostile takeover of Epiderm International, instantly transforming Derma into the largest in the industry. That caught Integume and All Nippon Cutis completely off guard. By the time they proposed buying SubCutis, that company's parent, All Nippon Cutis, was too broke not to capitulate.

Ultimately, however, it was brilliant marketing that invigorated them. "Why pretend? Slide into a genuine *american.* One is all you'll ever need." Sales picked up, thanks to their clever offer of low-interest, long-term loans. If you bought a top-of-the line, they threw in an Epiderm topskin or Sub-

Cutis accessory on layaway at a discount. They didn't have to lower prices or redesign their main line. Timing was all. Folks were sick to death of hype.

Well, I wasn't going to be left behind over something as important as skin. Skin-buying is something you do once in a purple sun, or at least, that's the way it used to be in my father's day, as he loves to remind me. Derma refinanced my debt with SubCutis and Epiderm. It made my millennium celebration.

I'd like to stay with *american* for awhile. You know, give myself time to get used to it. It fits well, neither too tight nor too loose. I still have faith in this classic model.

But the skin industry's so unpredictable these days.

Epiderm US launched two niche lines in time for Christmas, *indigo jazz* and *latin hues*, and sales were bigger than anyone predicted. Maybe they're not so niche. And how about that rash of IPOs of small companies in the middle of last year? Who would have thought the stock prices of Kimchee Kasings, Hide-the-Curry, and TagalogitPelts could triple by year-end? Some analysts think these upstarts could give Derma a run for their money. Nothing's what it seems anymore.

Also, People's PiFu has been making noises recently about going public here, saying they'll list on the New York Stock Exchange. Now that's earthshattering news in my books. They hired this youngish CEO a few years back—quite a change for them—and just launched a brand new product line, *sinokapitalist*. I like it. It's got a kind of postmodern pizzaz, something I can't quite define, that seems right for this century. Papa thinks it's ridiculous, although he grudgingly admits now that *china cutis* has run its course.

Let's just say I've learned from my fashion mistakes. Besides, for all we know, the next trend will be in chins, or something else equally unexpected. I'll wait a bit, to see how this new model fares, before I even think about exchanging my *american* skin.

CPSIA information can be obtained
at www.ICGtesting.com
Printed in the USA
BVHW040729311218
536764BV00012B/111/P